TO SILENCE THEM

DI SAM COBBS #2

M A COMLEY

*A very special thank you to the wonderful Clive Rowlandson, my special Facebook friend, who has allowed me to use his stunning photos of the Lake District as covers for this series.
I look forward to watching your future adventures, walking on the Fells with Alpha.*

ACKNOWLEDGMENTS

Special thanks as always go to @studioenp for their superb cover design expertise.

My heartfelt thanks go to my wonderful editor Emmy, my proofreaders Joseph, Barbara and Jacqueline for spotting all the lingering nits.

Thank you also to my amazing ARC group who help to keep me sane during this process.

Thank you to my good friends, Alex and Claire, for allowing me to use your names in this series.

To Mary, gone, but never forgotten. I hope you found the peace you were searching for my dear friend.

ALSO BY M A COMLEY

Blind Justice (Novella)

Cruel Justice (Book #1)

Mortal Justice (Novella)

Impeding Justice (Book #2)

Final Justice (Book #3)

Foul Justice (Book #4)

Guaranteed Justice (Book #5)

Ultimate Justice (Book #6)

Virtual Justice (Book #7)

Hostile Justice (Book #8)

Tortured Justice (Book #9)

Rough Justice (Book #10)

Dubious Justice (Book #11)

Calculated Justice (Book #12)

Twisted Justice (Book #13)

Justice at Christmas (Short Story)

Justice at Christmas 2 (novella)

Justice at Christmas 3 (novella)

Prime Justice (Book #14)

Heroic Justice (Book #15)

Shameful Justice (Book #16)

Immoral Justice (Book #17)

Toxic Justice (Book #18)

Overdue Justice (Book #19)

Unfair Justice (a 10,000 word short story)

Irrational Justice (a 10,000 word short story)

Seeking Justice (a 15,000 word novella)

Caring For Justice (a 24,000 word novella)

Savage Justice (a 17,000 word novella Featuring THE UNICORN)

Gone In Seconds (Justice Again series #1)

Ultimate Dilemma (Justice Again series #2)

Shot of Silence (Justice Again #3)

Taste of Fury (Justice Again #4)

Crying Shame (Justice Again #5)

To Die For (DI Sam Cobbs #1) Coming Dec 2021

Clever Deception (co-written by Linda S Prather)

Tragic Deception (co-written by Linda S Prather)

Sinful Deception (co-written by Linda S Prather)

Forever Watching You (DI Miranda Carr thriller)

Wrong Place (DI Sally Parker thriller #1)

No Hiding Place (DI Sally Parker thriller #2)

Cold Case (DI Sally Parker thriller#3)

Deadly Encounter (DI Sally Parker thriller #4)

Lost Innocence (DI Sally Parker thriller #5)

Goodbye, My Precious Child (DI Sally Parker #6)

The Missing Wife (DI Sally Parker #7) Out Feb 2022)

Web of Deceit (DI Sally Parker Novella with Tara Lyons)

The Missing Children (DI Kayli Bright #1)

Killer On The Run (DI Kayli Bright #2)

Hidden Agenda (DI Kayli Bright #3)

Murderous Betrayal (Kayli Bright #4)

Dying Breath (Kayli Bright #5)

Taken (Kayli Bright #6 coming March 2020)

The Hostage Takers (DI Kayli Bright Novella)

No Right to Kill (DI Sara Ramsey #1)

Killer Blow (DI Sara Ramsey #2)

The Dead Can't Speak (DI Sara Ramsey #3)

Deluded (DI Sara Ramsey #4)

The Murder Pact (DI Sara Ramsey #5)

Twisted Revenge (DI Sara Ramsey #6)

The Lies She Told (DI Sara Ramsey #7)

For The Love Of… (DI Sara Ramsey #8)

Run For Your Life (DI Sara Ramsey #9)

Cold Mercy (DI Sara Ramsey #10)

Sign of Evil (DI Sara Ramsey #11)

Indefensible (DI Sara Ramsey #12)

Locked Away (DI Sara Ramsey #13)

I Can See You (DI Sara Ramsey #14)

The Kill List (DI Sara Ramsey #15) coming March 2022

I Know The Truth (A psychological thriller)

She's Gone (A psychological thriller)

The Caller (co-written with Tara Lyons)

Evil In Disguise – a novel based on True events

Deadly Act (Hero series novella)

Torn Apart (Hero series #1)

End Result (Hero series #2)

In Plain Sight (Hero Series #3)

Double Jeopardy (Hero Series #4)

Criminal Actions (Hero Series #5)

Regrets Mean Nothing (Hero #6)

Prowlers (Hero #7)

Sole Intention (Intention series #1)

Grave Intention (Intention series #2)

Devious Intention (Intention #3)

Merry Widow (A Lorne Simpkins short story)

It's A Dog's Life (A Lorne Simpkins short story)

Cozy Mystery Series

Murder at the Wedding

Murder at the Hotel

Murder by the Sea

Death on the Coast

Death By Association

A Time To Heal (A Sweet Romance)

A Time For Change (A Sweet Romance)

High Spirits

The Temptation series (Romantic Suspense/New Adult Novellas)

Past Temptation

Lost Temptation

PROLOGUE

Fiona was on edge, as usual. Currently, she was sitting inside her car, alongside her husband, Rory, on the way to Buttermere for a rare day out. The sun had made a sporadic winter's day appearance at the end of February, and Rory had announced his intentions first thing, ordering her to get herself and their baby, Summer, ready within thirty minutes because he wanted to get on the road early.

She had raced around, collecting all the necessary items needed for a day trip out with a six-month-old baby, all under his watchful gaze and frequent sighing. He had made a point of following her from room to room, the way he had since their wedding day five years before. No matter what she said or did to appease him, he was always there, menacingly watching, within a few feet of her when he was at home.

"What brought this on today?" Fiona dared to ask.

"Does there have to be a reason for us to go out?" came his clipped response, silencing her.

Fiona rested her head back against the headrest and decided not to bother further. That's how it had been since the first day, their wedding day. He'd refused to let her move into his house before the marriage certificate had been signed. After the family get-together, he'd carried her over the threshold and whispered in her ear, "You're mine at last, to do with as I see fit."

She had been so loved-up at the time, she had misread the meaning in his words. That was her first mistake. He had raped her that day and every day after that until she'd announced her pregnancy. After that, he'd left her alone to enjoy her pregnancy without mistreating her in the bedroom.

Fiona had pleaded with the midwife to enforce upon Rory the need to give her time to heal after the baby was born—in other words, not to have sex for at least six weeks. Rory had smiled and nodded his understanding, but as soon as the midwife had left, he'd pounced on Fiona, swiping her across the face. He'd then roughly grabbed her around the throat and backed her up against the wall.

"You ever try that kind of trick again and you'll be sorry, you hear me?"

"What trick?" she'd choked out.

"Don't treat me like an idiot. I'll give you two weeks' recovery time."

Tears had emerged and trickled down her cheeks.

"Oh dear, have I made you cry?" he'd taunted.

Unable to swipe the tears away, furious that she'd displayed such weakness, she'd sniffled then whispered, "I'm sorry. I love you, Rory. Can't we start over? Live a normal life without—"

He'd tilted his head and sneered. "A normal life? What, like you being in my bed, like a normal, loving wife? Instead of me taking what is rightfully mine? Is that what you mean?"

She'd nodded.

He'd thrust his head towards her, his nose touching hers. "That'll be the day."

She was so caught up in her reverie that she neglected to hear what her husband was saying. He jabbed her in the leg.

"Did you hear me?"

"Sorry, I was too caught up, admiring the beautiful views. It's been ages since we went out exploring. I'm looking forward to today. Summer will revel in the fresh air as well."

"Shut up!"

"Sorry."

"You should be. What have I told you about only speaking when I give you permission?"

"I know, but... I thought today might be different."

"You mean you were *hoping* it would be different." He let out a menacing laugh that sent a chill rushing through her veins.

She gulped and remained silent, aware that what he'd said had been rhetorical.

The rest of the journey consisted of him glancing her way now and again and prodding her in the leg if she dared to peer out of the side window, instead of directly ahead of her.

"Almost there now. We'll have an hour's walk and then, if you're good, there's a café I think we should go to for some lunch."

"Sounds wonderful. Thank you for looking after us so well, I'm truly grateful." She was well versed in how to respond to his generous suggestions when they came. If she failed, she was also aware of what the consequences would be. Often, she would lie awake for hours, staring into the darkness of their bedroom, dreaming up ways of escaping her living nightmare. A nightmare she and her daughter were stuck in like quicksand. Could she allow her daughter, as she got older, to be subjected to such an horrendous lifestyle? Would Rory still treat her so harshly when their child was in her teens?

He had recently been talking about them having another child. She didn't have the courage to tell him she wasn't ready, either emotionally or physically, to even consider having a second child yet. What was the point? Going against his suggestions would only make matters worse for all of them. She loved her time alone with Summer when he was out at work. Even then, most days he surprised her during the day, to check up on her, making sure she was always busy, either keeping the house clean or tied to the kitchen, preparing and cooking an edible meal. Everything had to be freshly prepared with the best ingredients she could buy on the pittance he placed into her bank account on the first of every month.

She had only ever run out of money once. Never again, not after the thrashing she had received. Now, if there was any money left over, she hid it in a pot under her bed, her 'emergency escape fund' she called it. God help her if he ever found it. It hadn't really amounted to much, fifty pounds at the most so far, but it was fifty pounds towards her freedom. One day, soon, she hoped, it would help her and Summer to escape. The one thing preventing her, apart from the lack of funds already in place, was the knowledge he would hunt her down. Rory had threatened it often enough, to keep her on her toes, as if he knew what was going on inside her head.

"We're here. You get Summer, you can carry her while I take the rucksack."

"Okay." She knew the rucksack would be virtually empty: a few pieces of fruit, some formula for Summer, that's all. She was definitely getting the raw end of the deal. Summer was a healthy sixteen pounds now, which always seemed more like twenty when she was carrying her for more than ten minutes.

Rory parked up. "Get Summer ready, don't hang around either. I want to make the most of the fine weather."

Fiona glanced off into the distance, at the thick clouds shrouding the fells off to the right. She took Summer out of her car seat that was strapped into the back seat and placed her in the baby sling Fiona had only purchased the week before, after Rory had received a tip from a grateful customer of his.

They met up at the boot, and after Rory checked the straps were secure on the sling, they set off from the car up the steep incline. There were dozens of other climbers ahead of them and a few even returning to their cars. All of them spoke, saying a cheery hello as they passed. Rory, as usual, chose to ignore them, but Fiona always said hello with a happy smile. Much to Rory's annoyance. Yet, with so many people around, he knew better than to go on the attack and give her a good hiding.

They climbed and climbed; this was the first real bout of exercise Fiona had embarked upon since Summer's birth. She paused to rest for a few seconds. Rory tugged her arm, forcing her to plough on, to push through the discomfort, which she eventually did. After thirty minutes, the end was in sight, the small peak they were aiming to conquer. She glanced over to the right, thankful Rory hadn't chosen the other route as the vast hill disappeared into the clouds. No, this one was quite enough for someone trying to regain their fitness. The couple ahead of them paused to take the obligatory 'conquering the fell' photo and then headed towards them to make their descent.

Rory peered over Fiona's shoulder and then placed her and Summer on the edge of the peak, his arm wrapped around her waist, and he took a selfie on his mobile. "Smile for the camera, this could be the last picture we get of us together."

She frowned and turned to look at him and then nervously stared down at the huge drop behind them. "What are you saying?"

"Hush now." He squeezed her waist and angled her against him. "All will be revealed soon enough. Make a fuss and I'll kill you here and now."

"What?"

"What did I tell you?" He pinched her waist.

She yelped and stared down at the drop behind her again, as if mesmerised by the descent and the angles jutting out of the landscape. Fear continued to mount every second she was forced to remain in that treacherous position.

"Hey, come on, you're holding up the queue," a man shouted a few feet from them.

Relief swept through her when Rory's grip diminished and he tugged her behind him on their descent along the track, his words circulating through her mind as she trudged back down the hill and into the Skye Farm café, where he'd promised to buy them lunch.

Rory ordered for her, as usual. Their sandwiches arrived, a whole mini baguette filled with chicken, bacon and mayonnaise. It was delicious but far too big for Fiona to eat all in one go. She pushed her half-eaten lunch to the middle of the table.

He looked at the plate, then back up at her, and through clenched teeth, he ordered, "Eat it."

She put her flattened hand over her stomach. "I can't, I'm full."

He threw a serviette at her. "Wrap it up. You can have it for your tea later."

"Oh, okay." She wrapped the rest of her baguette in the napkin and handed it to him to put in the rucksack.

"Can't take you anywhere. Show you some kindness and you throw it back in my face every single fucking time," he said, seething.

She knew better than to retaliate, instead, she made a fuss of the gurgling Summer and sipped at her coffee. Straining an ear, she picked up on the conversation taking place behind her on the next table; it was regarding one of her favourite actors, Tom Cruise.

"Did you hear that?" she whispered forgetting the rule: not to speak unless he gave her permission.

"What? I don't listen to idle chitchat. Drink your coffee and we'll head off."

She sipped at her drink but still had one ear on the debate going on at the next table. "Excuse me," she took a punt and butted in, not daring to look in Rory's direction. "Did you say Tom was spotted around here lately?"

"That's right, love," a man in his fifties with a salt-and-pepper-coloured beard replied. "He was seen jumping out of a helicopter over the lake. Apparently, they were filming *Mission Impossible Seven* in the UK at different locations back in September. Nice chap, by all accounts. Friendly with the locals, didn't think twice about having his photo taken with them, not like some Hollywood actors. He does his own stunts, too, from what I've heard, not bad for a man around my age."

The rest of the table all laughed.

"Oh my, I think I would have died if he'd approached me, I'm one of his biggest fans."

"Have you finished?" Rory snapped.

"No, I've still got half my drink left," Fiona replied.

His face darkened. She stood her ground and sipped at her drink under his scowl, while still continuing her conversation with the man on the next table.

Rory's chair scraped on the flagstone floor, and he rose to his feet. "I'll be outside, don't be long."

"I take it your old man isn't a Cruise fan then," the bearded man said.

"No, you could say that. I'd better go, he gets a little moody if I keep him waiting too long. Nice chatting with you."

"You, too, love. Tell him to get a life and take a chill pill now and then."

Fiona laughed. After ensuring Summer was comfortable in her sling, she left the café and went in search of Rory who was standing up the slight incline at the front of the café. She smiled, hoping that would break down his barrier. It didn't.

"Ready?"

"Yes. Where are we going now?" She winced, remembering his rule.

"Home. I've had it with you embarrassing the hell out of me." He marched up the hill to the car, not bothering to look back to see if she was following him or not.

He revved the car engine as she finally opened the back door to put Summer into her car seat. She turned to see him staring at her in the rear-view mirror, his eyes narrowed. "Get a move on, we haven't got all day."

"But it's Sunday. I thought we were making a day of it." The fear was making her tongue slip far too often.

"We have. I've brought you out and you've ended up making a fool of me. What have I told you about talking to strange men? You never listen to me."

She closed the back door and hopped in the passenger seat. No sooner had she fastened her seatbelt, Rory reversed the car at speed onto the road. "Slow down, you almost hit that car. Don't forget Summer is in the back."

He yanked on the handbrake and glared at her. "Stop telling me what to do as if I'm some kind of novice driver. Button that smart mouth of yours, or you'll be sorry."

"I'm sorry. I was just saying—"

"Well, don't. How many times do I have to tell you? Keep quiet until you're spoken to. Don't engage in conversations with total strangers either, you can add that one to your list of things not to do."

"Okay. Calm down!"

His eyes widened in rage, and he jabbed the pointed fingers on his left hand into her thigh.

She yelled out in a mixture of pain and shock. "That hurt."

"It was supposed to. Now fucking button it."

She pulled an imaginary zip across her lips.

He set the car into Drive and put his foot down, nearly knocking down two irate walkers in the process who lashed out with their sticks at the rear of the car as Rory roared off. "Tossers, they should have been watching where they were going."

Fiona, too stunned to speak, stared ahead of her. He took a left at the bottom of the road. Fiona cringed when she read the sign; he was going to drive them to Keswick via Honister Pass. Her worst nightmare was about to happen. The thought of travelling the terrifying route again filled her with dread. Bile rose in her throat, along with her lunch. She dug deep to keep it from resurfacing, knowing that if she was sick at any point during the journey, he would pull over and make her clean up the mess.

Rory turned up the music, not caring if it disturbed Summer or not. All that mattered in his world were his needs.

Fiona's stomach felt on fire with the amount of bile stirring up a storm as the car approached the pass and they began the terrifying journey. Rory drove at breakneck speed during certain parts of the route, but when the necessity struck to slow down, he did, surprisingly. She tried to close her eyes, but that only made her feel far worse. At the very top, Rory drew onto a grass bank and ordered her to get out of the car. His words from their previous encounter on the fell at Buttermere resonated in her mind.

"Leave Summer in the car," he shouted.

"What if someone steals the car?" It was a dumb question, she knew that, but it was the first thing that popped into her mind.

"Look around you. We're the only ones up here."

His words and the wicked glint in his eye filled her with dread.

"Get out!" he barked again.

Unfastening her seatbelt, she reluctantly left the safety of the vehicle and peered in the back window to ensure her child was okay. *The keys are in the ignition, I could drive off. No, I couldn't, he's quicker than me.*

"Get over here. Stand with me and admire this fantastic view."

Fiona's steps were small and hesitant. Her legs trembled and her stomach twisted into a substantial knot. "Here's far enough. I can see the fantastic view just fine from here."

He reached for her, grabbed her arm and yanked her towards the edge. She was perilously balancing on her wobbly legs, trying to remain upright. Once she came to a standstill, he grabbed both of her arms and pushed her even closer to the ridge.

She screamed out, "Rory, don't do this. Think of our daughter growing up without me." *What about the other baby he wanted? Why has he changed his mind?*

"I do, every single fucking day. She'd be a much better person without you around."

"How can you say that? I'm the best mother I can be."

"Are you? Next, I suppose you're going to tell me you're the best wife ever to walk this earth, as well."

"No. I would never class myself as that, despite all the effort I put into making you happy. Don't do this. Let me get back in the car, please?"

Still grasping her arms, he inched closer still. A rock gave way beneath her feet, and she cried out a second time. Her gaze met his, and she pleaded with him, "Please, don't do this. I'll try to be better, work harder at home, to make both your lives the best they can be. I'm sorry if you believe I've failed you." Just then she spotted a car coming around the bend less than half a mile away.

What if he hears it approaching? Will he let me go? I can't bear this. Knowing he has my life in his hands. Please, God, help me!

1

"I shouldn't be late back tonight, Chris."

"How many times have I heard that over the years? Too many, that's how many."

Sam shook her head. She hated starting off her day with yet another falling-out with her husband, and this was definitely brewing up to be one of those days if his dark expression and the way he was tapping his finger against his mug was anything to go by. "You knew when you married me that my job meant a lot to me. Being an inspector in the Cumbria Constabulary is a vocation for me, not a career as such. Why can't you give me a break now and again?"

He slumped back in his chair and stared at her for what seemed like an eternity before he spoke. "That's all I ever hear from you. What about *my* job? It takes a lot of muscle and mental ability to be a landscape gardener. To come up with the best scheme possible for a client at the minimal cost. You know as well as I do how much the cost of materials has gone up since the pandemic started. I've had to go back to two clients I gave a quote to last year and tell them the quote is now twenty-five percent more. I thought one of the blokes was going to deck me. Furious he was, and I can't blame him, I'd be pissed off if a tradesman went back on his word with me."

"That's so unfair! I'm sorry you're having to contend with that crap. Why am I only hearing about it now, Chris?"

"Because it's my problem, not yours." He flung a hand up. "Anyway, the likelihood of you showing a blind bit of interest in my career is negligible, so what's the point?"

Sam sat there, her mouth dropping open in severe shock at the harshness of his words. It took her a second or two to recover. "Are you kidding me? We're a team, of course there would be a point in you confiding in me. I can't believe you can sit there and chuck that one at me."

"Believe it. Because all I hear, day in day out, is how hard *you* have it at work, as if nothing else in this world matters. I have to say, all this woe-is-me malarkey wears a tad thin after the first few times of hearing it."

"Bullshit! What utter crap you're talking." Sam glanced up at the clock on the wall in their new kitchen, the one they were due to pay off over the next five years, thanks to Chris ripping out the old one before they'd had a chance to either plan out the new design or got around to discussing whether they could actually afford a new one or not in the first place. That was Chris to a tee, though, go hell for leather with a project and sort out the consequences later. Lately, their marriage had been teetering on the rocks because they appeared to be going in different directions. Chris was desperate to have children—at times Sam wondered if he went out of his way to make life difficult for her, punishing her in some way for not falling pregnant, even after they had wasted their hard-earned money on five IVF treatments.

"Is it? Every night we have to discuss what's happened in your day. Do I ever get around to mentioning what my day has consisted of? Rarely. The second dinner is finished, you're upstairs, getting ready to go out with Sonny. That damn dog gets more attention than I ever get. Why? Isn't marriage supposed to be an equal partnership?"

"Of course it is. But taking on a dog is also a huge responsibility. He's by himself all day. I walk him before work and in the evening, it wouldn't be fair on him just to have a quick 'fetch the ball' in the back garden every day."

"Therefore, you're putting the dog's needs before mine."

"That's nonsense and you know it. You could always take Sonny to the park yourself once in a while."

He fidgeted in his seat. "He's your responsibility, you wanted the dog. We only got him because..."

His head dipped.

Sam knew it wasn't a good idea to mouth the words running through her mind, but she needed to get it out into the open once and for all. "Because I can't supply you with the kids you're so desperate to have. That's right, isn't it?"

He exhaled a large breath, and his head slowly rose to look at her. "Yes."

There, he'd finally admitted it, after all these years of her trying to worm it out of him. Not wishing to get into a full-on heated discussion about her failure to become a mother, she stood and cleared the breakfast things from the table. After doing the washing-up, she kissed him on the forehead and patted Sonny on the head. They then mumbled goodbye to each other and Sam left the house.

She found it incredibly hard to pinpoint how she felt at that moment. Hurt, angry, let down, bitter, defeated, a failure of grand proportions and, finally depressed seemed to sum it up. What a way to start your day. Sam slipped behind the steering wheel of her car and peered at the house over her shoulder, hoping Chris would have rushed to the front door with an apology on his lips. Nothing. He was nowhere to be seen. She indicated out of her spot and drove to Workington Police Station. She turned on the radio only to find 'their song' playing; she switched over the station as tears misted her eyes.

Don't let him get to you. He's the one with issues, not you, her inner voice enforced upon her. She felt like arguing with it, but what would be the point? Autopilot kicked in and, before she knew it, Sam was drawing up outside the station. Exiting the car, she collected her handbag from the passenger seat and nearly jumped out of her skin as someone blasted their horn behind her. Laying a hand over her racing heart, she turned to berate the person, but her expression softened when she saw who it was. "Bob Jones, you'll be the bloody death of me one of these days."

Her partner smiled and got out of the car. "Sorry, I thought you saw me pull in."

"I didn't."

"In a world of your own again?" His cheeky grin melted her icy heart.

"I keep telling you that you're a naturally gifted detective."

He inclined his head. His smile slipped, and a slight frown surfaced. "Everything all right, boss?"

She waved away his concerns. "Yep, fine. How are things between you and Abigail?" The last thing she wanted to do was burden her partner with her marital problems when he'd recently been through something similar in his own marriage. Thankfully, that was all sorted now.

"Couldn't be better. We've even been looking through holiday brochures. Who would have thought that would have been on the cards a few months back?"

Sam smiled and rubbed his arm as they walked towards the entrance of the station. "I'm delighted for you, Bob. You deserve all the happiness this world has to offer. You're one of the nicest men I know."

He stopped and turned to face her. "What's going on, Sam? It's not like you to hand out compliments like that first thing in the morning. Go on, hit me with it, I'm getting the sack, aren't I?"

She doubled up with laughter. "You really do brighten my day with your off-the-wall theories. Don't be daft. I'm being open and honest with you, that's all."

"Hmm... that kind of praise generally comes attached to a slap around the face, in my opinion."

"Let's get inside before these black clouds decide to piss on us." Pushing the door open, Sam said hi to the desk sergeant, Nick Travis. "Anything urgent come in, Nick?"

"All quiet overnight, ma'am. Looks like an easy day ahead for all of us."

"What the fuck did you say that for?" Bob was the first to say.

Nick cringed and shrugged. "It slipped out before I could engage my brain. I'll make a note on my pad, must try harder."

All three of them laughed.

"We'll head upstairs. Give us a shout if anything interesting comes your way, it'll give us a reprieve from doing all the paperwork we've got to tackle, wrapping up the last two cases we've solved."

"I hear you. I have paperwork coming out of my ears, too. I thought we were supposed to be turning into a paperless society."

"Yeah, I guess HQ didn't get the memo on that one." Sam chuckled and entered her code into the security pad.

Bob followed her through the door, and they wound their way up the concrete stairs to the incident room. They were the first of the team to arrive.

Bob did the honours of pouring the first cup of coffee for the day, leaving Sam to go through to her office to see what post awaited her. Thankfully, it consisted of only ten brown envelopes today.

"Looks like you'll be getting let off lightly today," Bob said, eyeing up the smaller-than-average pile.

"Fingers crossed. Saying that, it depends what crap lies within, doesn't it?"

"I suppose. Anything specific you want me to be getting on with?"

"I need you to keep on top of the rest of the team, ensure all their reports are on my desk at the end of the day at the latest. I sense something big is about to come our way soon."

"You always say that. I've lost count the number of times I've heard you utter those words over the past year or so."

She raised a finger. "Ah, but how many times have I been proved right?"

Bob laughed and rolled his eyes. "I'm dipping out of this debate before it gets too heated. I'll leave you to it."

"Thanks for the coffee, coward," she shouted after him.

"You're welcome," he called back.

Sam sighed, her equilibrium back on track, thanks to her fantastic partner. She settled behind her desk and ripped off the front sheet of her desktop calendar. She knew she was still living in the Dark Ages, when all she had to do to check the date was to open up her phone, but sometimes, she preferred to do things the old-fashioned way.

Halfway through the morning, Sam received an interesting call from the desk sergeant. "Hi, Nick. Please tell me you're about to save me from banging my head against the wall."

"Tough morning going through your paperwork, I take it?"

"And some. Go on, what can I do for you?"

"We've got reports of a missing person. I wondered if you'd be interested in taking on the case until something more substantial comes your way."

"Go on, let me have the details."

Nick filled her in, and her pen darted across the A4 pad she kept on her desk as he relayed the information. "Okay, I've got that. Bob and I will visit the address now, see how things lie."

"Good. Another one I can tick off my list. Thanks, ma'am."

"No problem." She rose from her seat and went in search of her partner. "Put what you're doing aside, you can finish it later, and come with me."

"Sounds ominous," Bob replied. He slipped into his jacket and followed her out of the incident room.

"How have things gone this morning?" she asked.

"Okay. I passed on your instructions, and everyone has had their head down doing their thing, even Alex."

"Blimey! No wisecracks from him this morning? That's got to be a first."

Bob laughed. "I didn't say that. I cut him dead when he started telling us his latest clutch of jokes. He soon got the message. Where are we going?"

"You'll find out soon enough. We're chasing up a missing person report."

"Eh? Not usually our domain, is it?"

To Silence Them

"I know, but I'm bowing to Nick's better judgement here. If he thinks we should be involved, then so be it."

"Okay, where are we going?"

Sam handed him the sheet of paper, and when they got in the car, Bob entered the postcode into the satnav and Sam set off. "I don't think we'll need that. The village is close to where I live, so I should know the way."

Fifteen minutes later, Sam drew up outside a small row of terraced houses; the one they were after was in the middle. All the properties were pebbledashed and showing signs of neglect. The front gardens all appeared to be overgrown—talk about keeping up with the Joneses.

Sam rang the bell. It didn't work, so she used the letterbox instead. A woman in her early thirties with tear-stained cheeks, holding a baby, answered the door.

Sam pushed down the need to reach out and hold the baby. "Mrs Knox?"

"That's right. Are you the police?" she asked, her tone terrified.

"Yes, I'm DI Sam Cobbs, and this is my partner, DS Bob Jones. Would it be okay if we came in?"

"Sorry, where are my manners? Yes, do come in. I'll just put Summer in her playpen, she'll be fine in there, that way we can talk without being disturbed."

Sam smiled and nodded. "Thanks. How old is Summer?"

"Six months. She's a treasure most of the time. Sleeps for eight hours solid. Sorry, I'm talking babies to you, that's not why you're here."

"In your own time. Is there somewhere we can wait while you deal with Summer?"

She pointed down the long, narrow hallway. "Last door on the right is the lounge. I won't be long."

Sam and Bob walked into the lounge and made themselves comfortable on the sofa. Sam surveyed the room. There were family photos in different coloured frames on every surface. The man in the photos was tall, dark, and what Sam would describe as ordinary-looking.

Fiona Knox entered the room and sat in one of the small armchairs which had seen better days. Sam wondered, as none of the furniture was matching, if it was either secondhand or had been donated from different family members. Fiona took a tissue from the box next to her and wrapped it around two of her fingers.

"Why don't you tell us when you last saw your husband?"

"On Sunday, we got home around two-thirty in the afternoon. He dropped me off, said he had to go and pick something up, and never came home. I've been out of my mind with worry ever since."

"Have you reported his disappearance to Missing Persons?"

"Yes. I did that this morning. Did I do the right thing? I looked it up on Google, and it said the police wouldn't be interested in getting involved if the person had been missing for less than twenty-four hours."

"In that case, may I ask why you didn't contact us yesterday afternoon, once the twenty-four hours had passed, if your husband is still missing?"

"I'm sorry. My daughter was sick yesterday, she was my priority. I had a doctor's appointment at four and couldn't bring myself to postpone it. She had sickness and, you know, kept filling her nappy every five minutes. That's a lot to deal with, as you can imagine."

"Sorry to hear that. Is she better now?"

"Yes, a hundred per cent better, only because the doctor prescribed some medicine. Thank goodness, one less thing to worry about."

"I feel for you, it must be hard juggling looking after your child and dealing with your husband's disappearance. Can you run through what happened on Sunday leading up to his disappearance?"

Fiona smiled and fidgeted a little in her seat. "Yes, of course. We went on a rare outing. It's been full-on since Summer was born; we've barely had any time to ourselves, in truth. Rory, that's my husband, he took us to Buttermere for the day, well, for a few hours anyway. We parked the car and climbed one of the smaller hills. Then he treated us to some lunch at the little café there. We then went back to the car and came over Honister Pass. We stopped at the top… to admire the view."

Sam noticed Fiona's gaze drop at this point. "Did something happen up there?"

"No. I'm not sure what you mean. We got out of the car, just like any other sightseer would, it's such a beautiful spot."

Sam decided not to force the issue, maybe she'd picked up on something that just wasn't significant enough to challenge further. "Were you up there for very long?"

After running a hand over her cheek, Fiona shook her head. "I'm trying to recall. I think it must have been about five to eight minutes. Rory isn't really one for taking in the views, not like me. He gets bored easily whereas I could have stayed there for the rest of the day, given the chance."

"It takes all sorts. And what happened then?" Sam glanced sideways to check her partner was making notes. He was.

"We drove home and unloaded the car. I was by the front door when he called through the passenger window, saying that he had to pop out and that he wouldn't be long. That's the last I saw of him."

Again, Fiona's gaze dropped, putting Sam's suspicion gene on red alert. "And he hasn't contacted you since? Have you tried ringing his mobile?"

"No, not heard from him since, and his mobile was here. He left it charging in the kitchen. I wasn't aware of that when we were out. He's not really one of these people who is glued to his phone, maybe at work, but not when he's at home with us. He doesn't really do social media either."

"Can I ask what your husband does for a living?" Sam asked.

"He's a painter and decorator. Don't bother looking around, I know our house is a mess. He's been promising to do it up for ages, then lockdown struck… and well, he didn't earn any money for months. Now he's inundated with work."

"Do you have a list of customers who he's worked for lately?"

"Yes, I can check through the invoices, if that will help?"

"It will. We'll also need to check out the upcoming appointments for this week, if you can supply those for us. Has your husband been under any form of stress of late?"

"Every self-employed person I know is stressed to the max since the pandemic began. We've struggled to make ends meet at times. The government did very little to help people like us when they were dishing out the billions during the lockdown. It took them a while to sort things out for us."

"I understand. But if that's the case, why should it affect your husband now when the restrictions for the pandemic have been lifted?"

"I'm not saying it has. You asked me if Rory had been under any form of stress, and I gave you my answer."

"Okay. Let's think about this for a few minutes. What make and model of car does he drive?"

"It's a Toyota Auris, a hybrid, we're doing our best for the environment. We've only had the car about a year or so, we bought it just before the pandemic struck. Do you want the plate number?"

"Yes, that would be helpful."

Fiona reeled it off without hesitating. Sam was amazed the woman could tell her, knowing full well that she wouldn't be able to inform someone of what Chris's reg was, if they asked. "Okay, we'll get that circulated ASAP. Is there anything else you can help us with? Was Rory in debt? Might he have got into gambling trouble, anything along those lines?"

"No, no, we just don't have the funds, not these days, for him to be involved in that type of thing."

"I'm trying to throw out scenarios which have been the cause of people disappearing in the past. Generally, the spouses are the last to know when there are huge gambling debts left behind."

Fiona seemed horrified at the suggestion. "Oh, no. Please don't tell me that, I don't know how I'm going to cope financially if he doesn't return as it is. Please, what do you think has happened to him? Could someone have hijacked his car on his way to running his errand? But if they had, why hasn't he found his own way back home by now?"

"It's a possibility. We're going to need you to fill in a lot of the blanks for us, to supply us with the information I've requested. I'll get my team to go through it all with a microscope and see what comes up. I'm going to also need to speak to your doctor; is he or she the family doctor?"

"Yes, Doctor Livesy, we've been with him for years now. He's at the Moorgate Surgery in Workington. Our local surgery closed down around four years ago, and we were transferred to them. Which suits me, I can usually do the shopping at the same time we have an appointment."

Sam nodded. "Makes sense. Do you own a car or are you reliant on public transport?"

"I have to rely on the buses keeping to their schedules most days. Now and then, Rory will take me into town to shop after he's finished work, not that often, though. Have you ever tried juggling three to four bags of groceries with a baby in your arms? Getting on and off a bus with a pram is an utter nightmare at the best of times, so I tend to put Summer in a sling and head off."

"It must be tough. I don't suppose people think about the complexities of motherhood when they're having their first child."

"I know I didn't. I wish I had a little runaround to call my own, the fact is, I haven't. Mainly because of the costs involved, what with me not working."

"Is it your intention to return to work?"

"No. Rory told me not to bother as we're going to have a lot of children, apparently." Her head dipped again.

"Would that be a joint decision?" Sam probed gently.

"I thought so at the time, except no one truly realises how much hard work looking after a baby twenty-four-seven really is."

"I can vouch for that," Bob chipped in.

"Do you have children, Inspector?" Fiona raised her head to ask.

"Sadly not, so you could say I'm out of my depth asking these sorts of questions, and you'll have to forgive me. What about friends and family? Have you tried contacting them to see if anyone has seen Rory?"

"I got in touch with his parents, it was a quick call, I didn't want to upset them any more than was necessary at this stage. They told me they hadn't heard from Rory in over a week, since we last visited them. They were kind enough to ask us around for Sunday dinner."

"And did you believe them?"

Fiona shrugged and locked gazes with Sam. "Yes, I had no reason to disbelieve them."

"And his friends? Have you rung any of them?"

"No, I couldn't bring myself to involve them, don't ask me why."

Sam smiled. "I'm sorry, but I'm going to have to ask why. Don't you get on with his friends?"

"Yes, sometimes. Not that he has many. Three good ones at the most."

"We'll need their names and phone numbers, if you wouldn't mind?"

She rose from her seat and left the room. A few minutes later Fiona returned carrying a mobile. "Sorry, I checked in on Summer to make sure she's all right. She's happily lying there with the teddy I gave her." She handed Sam the mobile. "I've unlocked it, it's my husband's phone. If it will help, you can take it with you."

"That would be great, thank you. I can get my team to do the necessary, it could prove to be the key that unlocks this particular puzzle."

"Good. Because I'm seriously at a loss to know why, or how, my husband could vanish like this."

"Is there anything else you can tell us? Has he had a problem with any of his customers? Someone neglecting to pay their bill?"

"No, not that I know of." Fiona sat in the armchair again. "I've been sitting here thinking all sorts, since I realised he was missing. Dark thoughts that don't belong in my head. What if he's lying injured somewhere? Had an accident and come off the road? I've rung all the hospitals I can think of within a twenty-mile radius, and none of them could tell me anything. Maybe you'll have better luck than me on that score."

"It'll be one of the first things I instruct my team to do when we get back to the station. It does seem strange that your husband has just vanished into thin air, with no reason behind his disappearance. Would you mind giving me the list of customers he's dealt with lately and possibly let me see his diary for the next few weeks ahead?" she repeated her request.

"No, sorry, I should have got the information for you already. I'll be a little while, the office is in the spare bedroom upstairs. Rory is a messy worker and hates me interfering in the office, so please bear with me."

"Take your time, we're here for as long as you need us to be."

"What about a drink?"

Sam nodded. "I'll make it. What would you like?"

"I'll just have an orange squash; trying to keep off the caffeine while I'm still breast-feeding Summer."

"Good idea." Sam followed Fiona out of the room. She pointed out where the kitchen was and then ran up the stairs to obtain the paperwork Sam needed.

Once in the kitchen, Sam filled the kettle and prepared two cups with coffee granules and sugar and then opened a few of the overhead cupboards, looking for a glass. On her third attempt, she found one and located the bottle of orange squash on the side close to the kettle. Sam glanced around the small but adequate kitchen. It was showing signs of neglect here and there, especially on the worktops. Strips on some of the edges were missing large chunks on the corners. There were white ring marks on the blue worktops where someone had likely placed a boiling-hot pan, instead of using a heat-resistant trivet or something similar.

Sam listened for Fiona coming back down the stairs and continued to snoop in the cupboards and in the fridge. The cupboards were reasonably full, but the fridge was lacking any fresh vegetables, although there were a few yogurts, a tray of eggs and some cheese in there, all sitting alongside two four-packs of lager.

The kettle clicked off. Sam took the milk from the fridge, added a little to the two mugs and returned it.

The stairs creaked as she carried a tray she'd found into the lounge. "Here we are. Fiona, orange for you, I hope I haven't made it too weak for you. Bob, a coffee, just how you like it with one sugar."

Bob screwed his nose up at her. He had a sweet tooth, usually had two, sometimes three sugars in his coffee. She did her best to cut him back when the option was open to her.

"Thanks, boss, you do look after me," he said, his reply laced with sarcasm.

Sam smiled and took her seat next to her partner. "How did you get on, Fiona?"

"Okay, I think. I just need to sort through his diary now, match up the appointments with the invoices, if that's all right?"

"Go for it. The more detailed information you can give us the better."

Fiona took a sip from her orange and then got on the floor and spread the paperwork out on the worn carpet. Within ten minutes, she had things sorted enough to hand over to Sam, who had just finished her mug of coffee and was putting it on the table beside her.

"Excellent. I'll flick through, see if I have any questions relating to the invoices before we leave."

"Of course. I'll try and help when and if I can."

Sam skimmed through the paperwork but found nothing out of the ordinary from what she could tell at first glance. "Cheeky question, would it be okay if we took this lot with us? We'll return it as soon as my team have examined things closely."

"Feel free. They're no use to me." Fiona then handed Sam the diary. "You said you wanted to see his schedule for the next two weeks. I'm presuming you'll find what you need in there. I had a quick look, and at the back, he's written out a list of his regulars with their phone numbers, maybe that will help you a little."

"That's brilliant and will no doubt save us a lot of work. Is there anything else you can think of that may help our investigation?"

She shook her head. "I can't think of anything. Do you think you'll find him?"

"Given time and a little investigative work, yes, I'm sure we will, providing he wants to be found, of course."

Fiona frowned. "Sorry, do you mind explaining what you mean by that?"

"Statistics tell us that a very small percentage of people who walk away from their families and home life do everything they can to avoid being found. I'm just warning you to be prepared in case that's what we're dealing with here."

"Oh, I see. I hadn't thought about things that way. Why do people take off and never return?"

"Pressure, stress of a situation. They feel overwhelmed, and rather than face reality they choose to throw in the towel on their old lives and start afresh elsewhere. I'm not for an instant saying that's the case with your husband, but it might be something we need to consider further down the line, if he doesn't return home in the next few days."

"I get that. I hope he does come home. I'm not sure how I'm going to cope without him being here. It's not like I can leave the baby and go to work myself, she needs me."

Sam inhaled then exhaled a large breath. "I think you're going to have to prepare yourself for doing just that, if he doesn't come back in the near future."

Fiona appeared shocked by the news. "My God, what will I do? I have no skills."

"What did you do before you became pregnant?"

"I sort of ran Rory's business from home. When I say that, I answered the phones and typed up the invoices when he needed me to. The last nine months or so, three months before Summer came along, he ordered me to stay out of the office. That's why it's a mess up there."

"Did you challenge him about that?"

Fiona's chin sank to her chest. "No. I didn't… it wasn't the done thing, not with Rory."

"Very possessive of his work, is that what you're telling me? Or was he conscious of not causing you too much stress with the baby on the way?"

"A bit of both, I suppose. It's hard to explain."

"Can you try? I know it feels like your whole world is crumbling around you, but at the moment, none of this is making sense, and we need to find out the reason behind your husband's unexpected disappearance. The only one who can assist us with that is you."

"I've tried my best. I've been searching my mind, but nothing is giving me any indication as to why he would run off. Unless..."

"Unless?" Sam asked, her interest notching up a level.

"Unless something terrible has happened to him. You need to help me find out. Can you do that?"

"We're going to do our very best for you. Do you have a mobile or a house phone?"

"Only a mobile. I don't think I've charged it in ages. No one contacts me, not really, not since I've had the baby. All my friends are single, the last thing they need is for me to be going on about baby problems."

If her husband is missing, you'd think she'd have charged it by now. Maybe she's still suffering from baby brain. "Who did you turn to when you needed to vent before you had Summer?"

"My best friend, Sophie. She's had a lot of issues of her own to deal with in the past few months, so I didn't want to add to her burden."

"Sophie what? I'm sure she wouldn't have minded, sometimes listening to a friend's problems can alleviate some of your own stresses and worries."

"Sophie Burrows. Yes, with some people, that's undoubtedly true. Not with Sophie, though. She caught Covid, you see, was knocking on death's door at one stage. Now she has what the doctors are calling long Covid. The disease aged her overnight. I would be selfish if I laid anything like this at her door."

"That's such a shame. What about your parents? Surely they would listen to your concerns, if you needed them to."

"Oh, they do, I just don't like to burden them too much with what goes on in my life."

"Isn't that what parents are for?" Sam reflected on her own situation. Most of the time, her parents were in the dark about the problems within her marriage.

"They're busy with their own lives. We pop around to see them at the weekend, but apart from that, we all tend to lead separate lives."

"But wouldn't they be mortified if you didn't tell them that Rory had gone missing?"

"I guess. I thought I would obtain some guidance from you as to what my next move should be. For instance, should I ring Rory's parents and tell them he's gone missing?"

"I thought you told us that you'd already rung his parents."

"I have, it was a quick call to see if they'd seen him. They hadn't. I made out it was me being silly and that I'd forgotten where he said he was going."

"And have they contacted you since?"

"No. They generally leave us to it."

"He's not what you'd call close to his family then?"

"Yes, I suppose he is. Oh, I don't know, all this is too much for me to try and get my head around. I'm probably talking a lot of nonsense, just trying to make sense of it all. Why would my husband just drive off and disappear one day?"

"Well, that's what we intend to find out. As I said when we arrived, the more questions we ask, the more insight we're likely to have about your situation."

"Is that it now? Have you asked me everything you need to know? Only I can't leave Summer alone for much longer, the last thing I need is for her to start kicking off."

"Okay, we're going to leave you to attend to your daughter now. If you give me your mobile number, I may have further questions for you later. I'll give you one of my cards so you can contact me if you think of anything else that may be of interest to us. How's that?"

"Sounds good to me." Fiona gave Bob her phone number and accepted the business card from Sam and then walked them back through the house to the front door. Attempting a smile, she said, "Thank you for taking me seriously. I didn't know who else to turn to."

"You're welcome. Hopefully, we'll be in touch soon with some good news for you."

"Or bad news if you find out anything, right? You won't keep it from me if you discover anything has gone wrong, will you?"

Sam inclined her head. "No, I promise you will be the first to know either way."

"Thank you, I appreciate that more than you know. Goodbye."

She closed the door, leaving Sam and Bob staring at each other, puzzled.

"Let's discuss this in the car," Sam whispered and turned on her heel.

Inside the vehicle, she faced her partner and asked, "What did you make of the interview?"

"Hard to tell. She seemed a little odd to me. What was your perception of her?"

Sam sighed and rested her head back. "In all honesty, I don't know. Something feels way off to me. Why leave it so long before contacting us about his disappearance? We need to check if her child was ill yesterday and go from there, I suspect."

"What's your gut telling you? That she's behind his disappearance?" Bob asked.

"Truthfully?"

"Yep."

Sam scratched her face and looked ahead of her. "One minute I'm feeling sorry for her and the next I'm thinking: what the hell are you up to, woman? What about you? What's your first impression of her and why we're here?"

"While I have severe doubts running through my mind, I can't say that I'm ready to point the finger in her direction, not yet."

"What's your reasoning behind that?"

"For a start, did you see the size of him in the photos? You know, compared to her. She's a wee dot, you think she's capable of hurting him?"

Sam inhaled a large breath. "You know as well as I do, Bob, if someone is determined enough to get rid of another person, they will find a means to do it. There are other ways of achieving their goal rather than getting their own hands dirty, have you thought about that?"

"A hitman?"

"Yes and no. What if they had fallen out of love with each other and she was carrying on with another man and he offered to bump him off so they could be together?" She faced her partner and added with a gasp, "Worse than that, what if the baby isn't his and the real father has done something to him? Maybe she's behind it all or perhaps she's an innocent party and genuinely doesn't have a clue what's going on."

"Jesus, and maybe you have a very vivid imagination that is running amok at present."

Sam nodded, smiled and turned the key in the ignition. "Yeah, maybe you've hit the sodding nail on the head. I'm at a loss to know in which direction this case is going right now."

"Where are we going to start?"

"First of all, I think we should get back to the station with the information Fiona has given us. I'll hand it over to the team to sift through, get them up and running ASAP. We'll have a swift coffee and then get on the road again."

"May I ask why?"

"I think we should see what the parents, from both sides, have to say about their marriage. We need to obtain the background details before we storm ahead in the wrong direction."

Bob heaved out a sigh beside her. "I totally get where you're going on this one. Maybe the parents will be more open with us?"

"Yep, that's my thinking as well. Although, saying that, it might be wishful thinking on my part. We'll see."

2

After organising the team, Sam arranged for Alex to put in a request to look through the ANPR and CCTV footage they had for the surrounding area close to the Knox house. That's all they had, after all. Fiona couldn't tell them in which direction her husband had gone or where his destination was. They had very little, to absolutely nothing, to go on. The rest of the team were instructed to ring the people on Rory's customer list and the customers who were booked in for jobs that week, to see if any of them had seen him in the past two days or if he'd made contact with them at all to cancel any imminent appointments.

Then, after grabbing a quick coffee, Sam and Bob hit the road again. "I think the best idea would be to pay Rory's parents a visit first."

"You're thinking he might be there?" Bob asked.

"Possibly. Or he might have contacted them."

"Hmm... we'll see."

"It's all we have at present."

. . .

Ten minutes later, they arrived at the semi-detached house on the edge of Workington. It was opposite a large park, and there was a small row of shops up one side of the street.

"Not been here before, have you?" Sam said.

"Nope, seems a good little community. The shops appear to be thriving at least, not run-down like the ones on the other side of the town, closer to the main supermarkets."

"I agree. Let's see what the parents have to say."

There was an old Ford Fiesta parked on the road outside the house. Sam pushed open the squeaky gate and walked up the cracked concrete path to the front door. A man with grey hair and a stoop opened it and frowned at them.

"Yes? Who are you? If you're selling anything you can do one, we're pensioners on a limited budget."

Sam smiled at the man and showed her ID. "We're DI Cobbs and DS Jones, Mr Knox. Would it be possible for us to come inside and speak with you?"

He motioned for Sam to hand over her ID and snatched it out of her hand. "Not until I check this out. Stay there." He slammed the door in their faces.

Sam and Bob stared at each other with raised eyebrows.

Bob chuckled. "That told you."

"Didn't it just?" Sam sensed that if Mr Knox finally relented and let them inside the property, they were in for a rough ride. She glanced up at the dark clouds overhead. "I hope it doesn't piss down."

"Bound to, now that you've mentioned it," Bob grumbled. He pulled his collar up around his neck as a breeze whistled down the street. This was swiftly followed by the downpour Sam had predicted.

Sam swore under her breath and knocked on the front door again. Mr Knox opened it, his ear to the phone, and nodded. "You can come in now. Don't blame me for keeping you standing out there in the rain, it's your mob who are to blame, they shouldn't have kept me on hold all that time. Well, come in then." He stepped behind the door, allowing them to enter, and handed Sam her warrant card back.

"Thanks. It doesn't matter, we're not fair-weather officers. Rain or shine, when duty calls, we dive in. I'm glad you felt the need to check out our credentials."

"Can't be too careful, not these days. There are dozens of scammers around. No need for me to tell you that, is there?"

"You're absolutely right to be cautious. I wish there were more people around as wary as you, Mr Knox."

He waved his hand. "Call me Stuart. What's this visit about?"

Sam removed her wet coat. He took it from her and hung it up on the hook by the large ornate mirror. "It's about your son, Rory."

Mr Knox eyed her warily. "Go on, what's he done?"

"Nothing, as far as we know. You're aware that he's gone missing, aren't you?"

"I was told he drove off on Sunday and hadn't returned. I admit we've been so up to our eyes in paperwork, sorting out our wills and putting our finances in place that we forgot all about him going missing. Shame on us. The mind at our age plays terrible tricks. My wife is suffering from dementia, some days she's good and other days she's really bad. Why don't we go through to the lounge?"

Sam's heart went out to the man who had visibly softened before her eyes.

"Sorry, where are my manners, would you like a drink? I was just about to make Cassandra and myself one, so it's no problem."

"No, we're fine. You go ahead, don't let us stop you."

He showed them into the lounge and introduced them to his wife who seemed dazed. "Cas, this is DI Dobbs and DS James. They've come to talk to us about Rory."

"That's nice. Take a seat." Cas smiled warmly and pointed at the sofa.

Sam didn't have the heart to tell Mr Knox that he had got their names wrong. He left the room, and an awkward silence descended. Mrs Knox sat in her chair next to the gas fire and continually nodded and smiled at them. She picked up a magazine, flicked through two or three pages and placed it in her lap, looked up and smiled, then put her reading glasses on the table beside her. She smiled again, picked up her glasses, turned over another couple of pages and put her glasses down again. Then she began the process all over again and again until her husband came back in the room with two cups of tea. He put one in her lap, on top of the magazine, and this appeared to put a stop to Mrs Knox's ritual.

"Why are they here?" Mrs Knox asked, deep lines developing in her brow.

"They're here to discuss Rory, love. Let's listen to what they have to say, shall we?"

Mrs Knox smiled at her husband. "Yes, that's an excellent idea, Raymond, let's do that."

Sam saw her husband flinch when she addressed him by another name, and her heart sank for him. Although he never corrected his wife, she could tell he was upset all the same.

He turned his attention to Sam and Bob, and after taking a sip of his drink, he asked, "What can we do for you? I take it he's still missing if you've shown up on our doorstep."

"It would appear so, yes. Your daughter-in-law called us today and has reported your son officially missing."

"But today is Tuesday, isn't it? Or am I mistaken? I never know what day it is."

"It is, sir. You say Fiona rang you on Sunday, is that right?"

"Yes. She told us Rory drove off and never came home again. She rang us a couple of times to see if he'd shown up here. I told her we hadn't seen him at all and that he hadn't called us. It's not like Rory at all." He rubbed his face and shook his head. "I feel guilty now for not chasing things up, I should've rung Fiona back to see if there was any further news. As I said, we've been up to our eyes in paperwork. I'm in the process of dealing with different power of attorneys for my wife. Do you have any idea how involved the forms are? I've had to get Ray and Babs next door in to witness things for me. Luckily, I got two sets of forms, because between us we managed to sign the wrong parts in one section. Anyway, enough about that, it's trivial in comparison, which is why I'm so bloody annoyed with myself."

"It sounds like you have enough going on as it is, sir, please don't punish yourself. Can I ask when you either spoke to, or saw your son, last?"

"He popped round to see how his mother was mid-week. He was decorating a house not far from here and at the end of the day popped his head in for five minutes. The briefest of visits, didn't even stay for a cuppa, which I thought was unusual. He just called in to see how his mother was." Tears swelled up in his eyes, and he brushed them away with his sleeve.

"Do you get any assistance, Stuart?" Sam asked.

"No, nothing at all. I'm pretty much here on my own, dealing with the situation twenty-four-seven. No one cares—let me rephrase that, no one in authority cares. Their answer is to put everyone with dementia into a home. I love Cas too much to put her through such an ordeal. My friend struggled to cope with her husband and finally gave in; he lasted a week in the home and gave up." He reached for his wife's hand, and her cheeks coloured up.

A large lump lodged itself in Sam's throat. She coughed to try to shift it. "I'm sorry to hear that. It must be hard with no support on hand. Does Rory help out?"

"Not really. He's got his own life to lead, has a young family to raise, and working full time doesn't give him a lot of spare time. He pops in on the odd weekend and during the week if he's passing the door, but that's about it."

"I see. May I ask when you last saw your son for a *proper* visit?"

"Let me think. Must have been a couple of weeks ago. He and his family came here for Sunday lunch, we prepared and cooked it together."

"The Sunday before last then, correct?" Sam asked just to make sure.

"That's right. Rory hinted they might go out for a surprise drive the following Sunday, which would have been two days ago. Now you say he's missing?" He shook his head in disbelief.

"Yes. When you last saw him, did he give you any indication that there was something wrong in his personal life?"

"Apart from the financial mess they've got themselves into, no, nothing else."

Sam raised an eyebrow. "Would you care to enlighten us regarding that?"

"Surely it's up to them to tell you, or Fiona at least. Didn't she mention it?"

Sam shrugged. "She told us money was tight, but it's my fault, I should have dug deeper. I didn't want to push things and upset her more than was necessary on our first visit."

"Understandable."

"Can you give me a little bit more information about their finances without betraying any confidences, perhaps?"

"Rory came to us cap in hand for ten thousand pounds." He let out a bitter chuckle. "I mean, look around us, the curtains are all faded, and the sofa is on its last legs, the TV comes and goes, the colour dips regularly during the day. If I had ten thousand floating around, I would use it to enhance our life a little more. Cas deserves that more than most. I just haven't got it, it's as simple as that."

"What was his reaction to the news?"

"He wasn't very happy. Stormed out of here after telling us that we'd always let him down. Which was a total lie. We've bailed our son out of his debts over the years, more times than I care to remember, and not once has he repaid us. How he had the audacity to fling that one at us, I'll never know."

"Do you have any other children, sir?"

"No, he's the only child. I know what you're thinking now, that we spoiled him as a youngster, but we didn't, not to our knowledge."

"I wasn't." Sam smiled. "What about other members of the family? Is he likely to turn to them for a cash injection?"

"Nope. I have a sister down in Torquay who wants nothing to do with us. He'd have to be desperate to go down there and knock on her door." His eyes widened. "You don't think he could have done that, do you?"

"There's only one way to find out. Would it be possible for you to give me her number and address?"

"Of course." He reached down beside him and withdrew an address book from the magazine rack. "Where is it now? Anna Saul, is it under A or S...? You can never tell. Ah, yes, under A, thought as much."

"Read it out, and Bob will make a note of the details," Sam replied.

"Okay, she lives at fifty five Oak Hill Rise in Torquay. Or she used to; like I say, we haven't been in touch for years. Do you want her phone number?"

"Yes, please."

He read it out slowly for Bob to jot down.

"Thanks, I've got that," Bob said.

"Is your sister married?"

"No, she's never been married. Ran her own beauty salon for years in Whitehaven, then decided to up sticks and move down south. Not seen her in years. We drifted apart, and neither one of us has had the gumption to get in touch. We were never what you would call close during our childhood."

"Is there a possibility that Rory might visit her?"

"Not in the slightest. I don't know where our son is. This isn't like him to just run off like this. Have you checked with his friends? Did he and Fiona fall out about something?"

"Not as far as we know. Fiona told us he dropped them off then said he had an errand to run. She hasn't seen or heard from him since. We've got a couple of friends to check with. Do you know if he's close to anyone in particular?"

Stuart thought the possibility over for a moment or two. "He used to be close to Mick, don't go asking me what his surname is, but that was maybe ten years ago. I have to say, I haven't really heard him mention Mick recently."

"Bob, make a note, and I'll give Fiona a call regarding that later. I don't recall that name being on the list she gave us."

Her partner scribbled the name down on a clean sheet of paper in his notebook.

"Who are these people, Stuart?" Mrs Knox asked warily, her gaze darting between the three of them.

"They're from the police, love, they're here about Rory." Stuart patted his wife's hand patiently.

To Silence Them

"Ah, Rory, I love my son so much. He's a terrible teenager, though, always getting into mischief that one, but we forgive him, don't we? It's what we do with our kids. They mess up and we forgive. What he needs is a good woman beside him. I hope he finds someone nice soon."

Stuart glanced at Sam and rolled his eyes. He patted his wife's hand again and said, "There's hope for him yet, love."

Sam knew she had to be guarded in what she said next, the last thing she wanted to do was cause Mrs Knox any discomfort. "Okay, I'm going to leave it there for now and give you one of my cards. If you hear from him, will you let me know?"

"I will."

She stood. Bob flipped his notebook shut and did the same. Mr Knox showed them back to the front door.

"I'm so sorry you had to witness that. She picks up on the slightest thing and then goes back ten, maybe twenty years or more. It's like she's living in a different decade at times."

"It must be extremely hard for you to have to deal with."

"It is at times, even more so when I have no other support. I'm not sure what's going on with my son, there must be a reason he's taken off. Maybe he's in deeper money trouble than I realised. Either way, what with caring for my wife, I don't have the brain space to deal with other people's issues. I know he's my son, but at the end of the day, he's thirty-two now, old enough to stand on his own two feet. I have too much to deal with here to become personally involved in my son's dramas. Harsh, but true, I'm afraid."

Sam retrieved her coat, stepped out of the front door and turned back to smile at Stuart. "Please, try not to worry about your son, we're going to do our very best to find him. Take care of yourself and Mrs Knox, sir. Thank you for seeing us today."

He shrugged. "Waste of your time, I know. But Rory must have had his reasons for disappearing the way he has. I'm just sorry I couldn't tell you more. Maybe he's purposefully kept me in the dark, except for asking me for money, of course. Do people go missing when they owe a lot of money?"

Sam tutted. "Sadly, yes, they do. Saying that, they usually pack up their belongings before they consider leaving the family home. That's what is puzzling us with Rory, he appeared to have just simply walked away."

"Send my regards to Fiona, she doesn't deserve this. I'll try and give her a ring later, but my hands are pretty much full for most of the day, and my own memory isn't quite what it used to be."

"Don't worry, I'll pass a message to her when I ring her next. Thank you for your time. I'm sorry if we confused your wife by visiting you."

He smiled. "I assure you, it doesn't take much. My advice to you would be to never grow old. It's not much fun if you have to live with someone with dementia day in and day out. I find myself clinging to the old days, we were so much in love."

A couple of drops of rain dripped down her neck from the gutter over the door. "So sorry. We won't keep you, sir. Thank you for your time."

"If my son gets in touch, I'll ring you. Goodbye."

He closed the door, and Sam blew out the breath she'd been holding in and walked towards the car. "Bloody heartbreaking, isn't it? We don't realise how well off we are until we see what others have to deal with on a daily basis."

Bob cleared his throat before he spoke. Sam could tell he was feeling every bit as emotional as her. "Soul-destroying to see that woman like that. To see the love he has for her was truly touching."

Sam shook her arms out, her way of relieving the stress running through her veins. "I agree. Come on, let's set that aside for now. We need to visit Fiona's parents now, hopefully get some insight into what we're dealing with, what state their marriage is in."

"Makes sense to me."

The Chanters lived on the opposite side of the town. The drive through the heavy lunchtime traffic gave Sam time to contemplate the case further. "Bob, do me a favour, call Claire and ask her to delve into the financial side of things. His bank accounts, both personal and business. Ask her to check the paperwork we left behind, see if there's anything in there about the suppliers he uses and give them a call, see if he has any outstanding debts with any of them."

"Will do. You think that's the key to this one? The money?"

"Hard to say right now. We should deal with it from the start, though. Let's see how much debt he was in first, and then we'll be able to form a better judgement. The thing that is niggling me is the fact that he just took off without even packing a bag. How many people do you know who would likely do that?"

"Not many, there again, we haven't got a clue what's going on in his head. People under severe stress do the strangest things, experience tells us that much."

"You're right. Okay, when you've rung Claire, can you then contact the surgery? Check to see if Fiona had an appointment yesterday for the little one."

"On it now."

Sam switched off from Bob making the calls and reflected on what they had learned so far, which didn't really amount to much. She drew up outside a large detached house in a quiet cul-de-sac a few minutes later. The rain was still heavy, and she and Bob dashed to the house which thankfully had a small porch over the front door to give them shelter. Bob rang the bell, and the door was opened by a slim woman in her sixties.

"Hello, can I help?"

Sam and Bob offered up their IDs. "DI Cobbs and DS Jones, would it be okay if we came in to speak with you for a few minutes, Mrs Chanters?"

"The police? What on earth would the police need to speak to me about?"

Sam smiled. "It would be better inside, if you don't mind?"

"But I do. Tell me what this is about."

"Your son-in-law, Rory."

"I've only got the one, thank goodness. He's more than enough for us to handle most days, I can assure you."

"Oh... would you care to elucidate on that for us? Inside, possibly?"

She sighed and took a step back. "Very well."

After removing their coats, Sam and Bob followed the woman into a very neat lounge. There appeared to be nothing out of place, and everything gleamed under the light when Mrs Chanters switched it on. "Too dark today, damn weather. Please, sit down and tell me what this is all about."

"Thank you. Are you aware that your son-in-law has been reported missing by your daughter?"

"I am. Have you found him yet? Bloody idiot, causing my daughter to get stressed out like this. Irresponsible nitwit, that's what he is."

"You're talking about him disappearing on Sunday, I take it?"

"Yes." Her tone was clipped, and she shuffled in her seat, looking uncomfortable.

"Is there something else you want to tell us, Mrs Chanters?"

Her gaze dropped to the floor then up to a wedding photo of Fiona and Rory, sitting on the sideboard, and then down to the floor again. Sam braced herself for what she anticipated was about to come her way. Only Mrs Chanters remained silent for a long time.

"Mrs Chanters, I'm sensing you have a lot to tell us, but are unsure how to proceed, am I right?"

She nodded slowly. "Yes, I don't like to speak ill of anybody, especially someone who is linked to my family by marriage, however, I think you should know the truth. Forgive me, but it's very difficult to form the words. I feel like I've failed my daughter... have done for years. Each time I tried to speak with her about the issue, she clammed up. There's only so many times you can reach out to someone in distress, isn't there?"

"That's true. Why don't you just come out and tell us what you know? We can work through the issues later."

Again, her gaze took in the wedding photo. She stared at it for a long time, constantly shaking her head. "She should never have married him. The signs were there in the lead-up to the wedding, but

Fiona was so in love with the idea of having a grand wedding and all the trimmings that she failed to see what he was really like."

Sam tensed up, waiting for her to continue. "Go on. Please, we need to know more about Rory's character and the reasons behind him taking off the way he has."

Mrs Chanters sighed heavily. "He's a monster, that's what he is. A *bloody monster*."

"You're not making any sense, that's not the impression we got from Fiona. Please, can you enlighten us further?"

She closed her eyes and shook her head, clearly searching for the right words. Finally, she revealed the truth. "He abuses her, both mentally and physically. I've been round there some days when she was too afraid to look in the mirror. Black and blue from numerous bashings, one after the other. The only time he didn't abuse her was when she was pregnant, only because he wanted children so much. That's the only reason he's with her, it's not because he loves her."

Bloody hell. "Oh, well, I have to say that's come as a total shock to me. Speaking with Fiona earlier I could tell something wasn't quite right, but this revelation has come out of the blue. Can you tell me when the abuse started?"

"On their wedding night... no, it was before that. During the wedding arrangements period, she wanted something one way and he was desperate to have it another way. He always won in the end, of course."

"Did your daughter confide in you?"

Mrs Chanters' chin dipped to her chest, and tears slipped into her lap. "No, never, I wish she had."

"May I ask how you found out about the abuse?"

"It wasn't until we went shopping for the wedding dress. I think, in all her excitement, she forgot the bruises were there. I gasped when I saw her torso covered in them. I verbally tore her to pieces there and then. It was wrong of me to do that. I was so shocked, you see. I should have probed gently, I'm aware of that; hindsight is a wonderful thing."

"Did you and your daughter have a conversation about the abuse?"

"Sort of. Once I'd calmed down, I tried to get it out of her how long it had been going on, and she said for a while. I couldn't fathom why she would stay with a monster like that. I suppose that old adage of love being blind comes into play. I felt sick seeing all those bruises. Who gives men the right to control their partners with their fists?"

"I'm getting the impression that you confronted him about the abuse."

"Too bloody right I did. And do you want to know how that went down?"

"Yes, please." Sam smiled at the now irate woman.

"My daughter stopped speaking to me for over six months. That, in itself, broke me into pieces. We sorted it out in the end. I had to agree never to raise the subject again."

"When you sorted things out with your daughter, were you alone?"

She closed her eyes momentarily and shuddered then opened them again and said, "Nope. He refused to leave the room. He had his arm wrapped around her shoulders the whole time she was trying to tell me that she adored him, loved him more than life itself and was blissfully happy with him. Good job my Phil wasn't in the same room, he would have battered the life out of him. They chose to tell me when Phil was away on a fishing trip with his friends. I felt violently sick when I left the house that day. Coming face to face with such an abusive man like that." She wiped her eyes on a tissue. "I'm one of the strongest women I know, but that day, even I shrivelled beneath his evil gaze."

"What a terrible ordeal for you. Since that experience, have you made it up with the pair of them?"

"Oh, yes. It was either accept the situation or never see my daughter again. He made it perfectly clear who was in charge. It was his way or the highway."

"And how have things been between them lately, do you know?"

"He's crafty, always left bruises where no one else was likely to see them. I caught her wincing as she sat down last week. We were in a coffee shop, she said she had a tummy ache. I didn't believe her one iota. How could I? Knowing the bloody truth. No woman should have to lead a life of utter misery like that."

"I wholeheartedly agree with you. Of course, when we visited your daughter earlier, she mentioned nothing about the abuse, which is understandable in the circumstances. Can you tell us anything else about their marriage?"

"Isn't that enough? He controls what she says and does, what she eats and drinks. If I was in her situation, I'd be bloody relieved that he's gone."

"Do you think that's why your daughter delayed reporting him missing? Most people ring the hotline after the twenty-four hours is up; your daughter contacted us almost forty hours after Rory disappeared."

"I can't speak for my daughter. I suppose she's reeling with confusion right now. She rang me on Sunday evening to say he'd driven off but she didn't seem too concerned. I might be doing her an injustice there, she cut the call short because she had to attend to my granddaughter."

"This is a very tough question to ask, so forgive me, but do you think Rory has ever laid a hand on Summer?"

She gasped and slapped a hand against her face. "Good God, I hope not. I would think Fiona's mothering instinct would come into force and she would do everything in her power to protect her daughter, if he'd even tried to lay a hand on Summer."

Maybe Fiona took things further and is guilty of getting rid of her husband.

"Can you tell me if your daughter has ever retaliated?"

Lynne's brow knitted into a deep frown. "No, I can't say for certain but I don't think my daughter has it in her to strike him back or to even shout at him. What makes you ask?"

"Just something that entered my mind. Everyone reaches a breaking point at some time in their life."

"I suppose. But she wouldn't have done it, not with Summer around."

"Yes, I understand. Having Summer around could go two ways, though: either stifle your daughter's reaction to her husband, or it could bring out the protective lioness in her."

Lynne considered the options for a while and then replied, "Definitely the former in my daughter's case. She would do anything and everything to live a quiet life."

"And yet, she remained living with an abuser."

"Yes. We didn't really discuss it. She made it clear it wasn't a topic she wanted to talk about. There are some women who seem to be put under a spell by their abusive partners. I've done my research on the subject, and my findings shocked me. For instance, the number of women who see domestic violence as the norm is horrendous, even if they end up in hospital fighting for their lives. They rebel against family members, accusing them of not knowing their partners or husbands, the abusers, as well as they do. Not that Fiona has ever come right out and said that." She shook her head. "Why take off like this? What the hell is running through that man's twisted mind now? Do you think he's punishing Fiona?"

Sam sighed and shrugged. "In all honesty, this case has flummoxed me. Maybe we'll get to the bottom of things soon, after speaking to more family members and his friends."

"Ha, if he had any. He was always hard to work out, that one. I can't tell you how much I'm glad he's gone, though, saying that, I'd want to know what has happened to him out of curiosity all the same."

"Has he ever shown any abuse towards you or your husband?"

"He's always had a sharp tongue in his head. Treated me like something he stepped in, that kind of thing. I tried to make sure I was never left alone with him. Phil, that's my husband, he's never really had anything good to say about him from the outset. Said there was something strange about him that he found hard to work out."

"And your husband knows about the abuse, I take it?"

"Yes. We sat down and talked long and hard about it one day, and he warned me not to get involved. His thinking was if we didn't know the facts, then we wouldn't drive ourselves into an early grave worrying about Fiona. In other words, she'd made her bed, and it was up to her to deal with the consequences."

"I see. And that goes against what you believe, right?"

"Oh, yes. God, if everyone gave up on their children, what type of cruel world would we be living in? Isn't it nasty enough already?"

"It is. Do you have any other children?"

"Yes, another daughter, Donna. She lives in a flat in Workington."

"Alone, or is she involved with anyone at this time?"

"No. She's decided to get ahead with her career, put any kind of relationship on hold until she's financially stable and able to stand on her own two feet, as it were. She's doing exceptionally well in that respect, too, she's already obtained two promotions within the past twelve months."

Sam could see how proud she was of Donna. "How exciting. What job does she have?"

"She works at a pharmaceutical firm. Don't ask me what her role is now, I've lost track. I know I shouldn't say this, but she really is the brightest of the two girls, always was throughout school. We're super proud of Donna's achievements."

"Do your daughters get along?" Sam asked, feeling more and more confused as to where this form of questioning was leading her.

"Oh yes. But when it suits. Donna won't take any shit—sorry for swearing—any crap from Rory. She sees him for what he is, a coward for striking a woman. When it all came out in the open, she took off before I could stop her. Drove round to Fiona's house, gave them both a piece of her mind."

Sam winced. "I take it the outcome wasn't good."

"Nope. She and Fiona didn't speak for bloody months. In the end, I had to trick them both. Told each of them to meet me for a coffee in town. Neither was happy when the other one showed up. I forced them to speak to each other, to work out their differences for the family's sake, and they did."

"When was this?"

"A good few months ago, I suppose."

"And they've been all right towards each other ever since?"

Lynne waved her head from side to side. "Sort of, with the strict instructions that Fiona's abuse issues were never discussed again."

"That must have been tough for Donna to deal with, knowing how angry she must have felt at the time."

"Yes, it was truly difficult for her, but she was prepared to go along with Fiona's wishes to remain in contact with her sister. It didn't mean she didn't hate Rory for the way he had mistreated Fiona, though. Donna could never forgive and forget him laying a hand on Fiona."

"We wouldn't mind having a chat with Donna. Can you give us her address and phone number?"

Another puzzled expression distorted Lynne's lined face. "May I ask why?"

"We believe in getting everyone's side of events, that's all."

"Ah, you think I'm exaggerating, is that it?"

Sam smiled. "Not in the slightest. The more people we speak to, the more likely it is that we will form a clearer picture of what we're dealing with."

"Okay, I can understand that. Let me get her mobile number for you." She scrolled through her phone and read out the number for Bob to make a note of, then also gave him Donna's address.

"Thanks, that's great. Is there anything else you think we should know?"

Lynne's mouth turned down at the sides, and she shook her head. "Not that I can think of. Have you checked his parents' house? Maybe he's hiding out there for a few days. Who knows what goes on in that head of his when he isn't striking out with his fists?"

"He's not there. Don't worry, I'm sure he'll surface soon. Thanks for your time. We won't hold you up any longer."

Lynne groaned as she stood and rubbed her hip. "Damn arthritis at my age."

"It looks painful."

"It is, I can assure you. I hope you find out all the information you're searching for soon."

"It was nice to meet you, and thank you for being so open with us, Lynne."

"Always the best policy in my opinion. Liars always get found out in the end, don't they?"

"If their memory isn't up to the task, yes, that happens all the time. Take care."

Sam and Bob slipped on their coats, left the house and walked back to the car. Once there, Sam glanced over her shoulder to see Lynne still standing at the door. "Don't say anything until we've driven away, we're being watched." Sam gave the woman a quick wave, jumped into the car and started the engine. They passed the house, and Lynne was still waving at them. "Not sure what I make of all that, what about you?"

"I'm reserving judgement at the moment. What's troubling you in particular?"

"He was clearly hated by Lynne and Donna. Maybe Fiona finally found the courage from somewhere and asked for help from her mother and sister, and they decided to get rid of him."

"Seriously? You came to that conclusion after one conversation?"

"What else do we have on the table at the moment? Nothing, right? So why not think of the obvious?"

"Obvious to you, maybe. I didn't get the impression that Lynne was trying to cover something up. No shifty behaviour or anything of that nature."

"No, you're right, in her case. However, when we were talking to Fiona earlier, there was something off about the way she spoke to us. Something I can't put my finger on."

"Ah, I think I might have the answer for you there."

Sam turned to see her partner beaming. "Go on then, smartarse. Give it to me."

"Think about it, when we interviewed Fiona, we weren't aware that she had been abused by her husband."

Sam looked at the road again, at the traffic building up ahead. "Hmm... okay, I'll give you that one. And you think that's why she seemed uncomfortable?"

"Yes, it adds up to me."

"I'm not getting that vibe at all, I have to say. There's a nagging voice at the back of my mind telling me that she's to blame for her husband's disappearance, and until I discover any evidence to the contrary, I'm going to stick to my guns on this one."

"That's your prerogative, but without any evidence backing up your suspicions, we're... how shall I put this...? Ah yes, fucked!"

Sam laughed. She could always rely on Bob to bring the tone of the conversation down to sewer level. "You're an idiot."

"Yeah, you've told me dozens of times over the years. Where are we going now?"

"I need to speak to the sister, thought I'd take a punt and show up at her work rather than ring her."

"Any particular reason?" Bob queried.

"You know I prefer gauging people's reactions in person rather than tackle them over the phone, where at all possible."

"Yeah, I had a feeling you were going to spout that one."

"Anyway, I think Sidwells is just around the corner, isn't it?"

"It is. It's that large white building we can see on the horizon."

"I thought it was. That settles it then." Sam gave her partner a satisfied grin.

He rolled his eyes and turned up the radio and then quickly lowered it again. "Can't stand the damn Carpenters."

"What? Are you mad? She had the voice of an angel."

"Maybe she did. Tell me this, have you ever listened to the words of her songs?"

"Of course I have, numpty, I always sing along to them."

"All right, I used to do the same until Abigail highlighted something a couple of months ago."

"What was that?"

"How depressing the words are in their later songs."

Sam laughed. "Don't talk wet. What are you like?"

"I swear it's true. Have a look on the web at the lyrics."

"I'll do that. You know she had anorexia, don't you? Although her actual cause of death was noted down as heart failure. Sad all the same."

"Yes, and isn't it regarded as a form of mental illness these days? I think back then, they saw it only as an eating disorder. And yes, I agree, very tragic. Since Abigail pointed it out, I haven't been able to listen to any of their songs."

"That surprises me, never had you down as the emotional type, Bob."

"Certain things have got to me over the years, not much, I have to admit."

"You give me something new about you every single day, matey. Don't ever change. There aren't many men in this world who are willing to show an emotional side to their nature."

"Don't you go telling tales on me now. What's said in this car stays in the car, you hear me?"

She chuckled and patted his knee. "Your secret is safe with me."

Sam took a right and then a sharp left and pulled up outside a security gate leading into the car park surrounding Sidwells.

A guard in a peaked cap approached the vehicle. "Can I help?"

"We'd like to see Donna Chanters." Sam showed him her ID.

"Is she expecting you?"

"No. We're hoping to question her in regard to an ongoing investigation."

"Okay, I'll have to check with her. We don't usually allow visitors not connected with the industry to enter the premises. I'm sure you can understand that rule."

"I can. If you can tell her, it's important that we see her today. Thanks."

"I'll be back in a second or two. That's if she's at her desk and not patrolling the plant."

Sam held up her crossed fingers.

The guard went into his little hut and emerged a few moments later, smiling. "She'll meet you at the main entrance. Follow the road around to the left, you should be able to park your car somewhere around there, it's not too busy today. Some days are more hectic than others."

"Thanks for your help, Stewart." Sam spotted the man's name badge, and he grinned from ear to ear.

"My pleasure."

Sam followed the guard's instructions through the massive car park which was around ninety percent empty. "Have you ever been here before?"

"Nope, can't say I have. Didn't realise this place was as big as this. You live and learn."

"Me neither. This should do us." She parked in a spot close to the entrance.

They exited the car and strolled over to the building. Before they made it to the entrance, a young woman wearing a knee-length skirt and an open white medical coat appeared.

Sam smiled and offered her ID. "DI Sam Cobbs, and this is my partner, DS Bob Jones. Am I right in assuming you are Donna Chanters?"

"You are. What's this about?"

"Is there somewhere we can talk in private?"

"Let me see what I can do. Step inside."

They entered the building, and Donna had a quick word with the doorman. He pointed over to the left, and Donna gestured for Sam and Bob to follow her across the extensive marbled hallway to an office. Surrounding the office was glass, on all sides and overhead, extending up several stories beyond the large sweeping staircase. Over to the right was a bank of five lifts, emphasising the size of the building.

"Come in and take a seat. It's adequate, nothing fancy."

Sam nodded. "It'll serve its purpose, thank you."

Chairs scraped on the marble flooring as they sat. Bob took out his notebook and pen, poised for action.

"I suppose my first question would be, what's this all about?" Donna queried.

"Have you had any contact with your sister in the past few days?"

"Yes, of course. She rang me on Sunday, she was beside herself, told me that her husband had gone missing. I haven't heard from her since. Why? Has something happened to her?" She wiped a hand over her cheek.

"Your sister formally reported your brother-in-law missing this morning." Sam noticed the way the woman cringed.

"Do you have to call him that?"

Sam frowned. "Isn't he? Aren't they married?"

Donna sat back and tipped her head up to the panelled ceiling. "I suppose so. I never really class him as that, not really."

"May I ask why?"

"Because I can't stand the man." She sat forward again and clenched her hands tightly. "There, I've said it out loud to the police. I'm glad he's missing. He's a vile man who should have been locked up years ago, in my opinion."

Sam noted the vindictive tone Donna had used. "Surely, if the man is married to your sister, you would be wise to make an effort with him, wouldn't you?"

"Oh, I do. My sister and I fell out a while ago because I was so furious with him."

"Why?"

She fell silent, as if struggling to find the right words. "Like I said, he's a despicable man."

"Okay, I'm going to come clean with you about something: we're aware of the abuse your sister has suffered."

"Phew, I'm glad you know. I can breathe more easily now. I didn't want to discuss the matter if you weren't privy to the information. Like I said, he's a revolting, and I'll even add, a truly exceptionally wicked man. Some men shouldn't be allowed to walk this earth. I heard the other day on the news that one woman dies every three days through suspicious circumstances in the UK. What the actual fuck? How is that possible? More to the point, what are the sodding police doing about tackling the bloody issue?"

"It's a dreadful statistic. I have to tell you that my team and I are doing our very best to deal with these cases thoroughly, when they're brought to our attention."

"Good, and so you should."

"Do you have any idea where Rory might be?"

Donna flinched at the sound of his name. "Nope, good riddance to the bastard. All I'll say is, he was selfish to the end, taking the frigging car with him."

"To the end?" Sam asked, searching for clarification.

"The day he walked out. My sister's life will be a trillion times better now he's off the scene. She's upset about his departure, but she'll soon realise that not having him around will give her and Summer the freedom to live a normal life."

Sam inclined her head. "Do you know what's happened to him, Donna?"

She banged her flattened hand on the table. "Of course I don't. I'm relieved every day he's missing for *her* sake. Go back there and ask her if she's slept well since he left, I bet she has. She hasn't had a good night's sleep in years, lying next to that creep, being at his beck and call twenty-four hours a day."

"Are you telling us you believe he raped her?"

"Call it what you like, not that the police would be interested. I know your lot don't regard it as rape when a couple is married."

Sam raised a hand. "I'm sorry, I have to refute that. We take allegations of abuse within a marriage very seriously indeed. If it's reported to us. Was it?"

Donna shook her head and hung it low. "No, she refused to do it. I tried my hardest to persuade her, but it was pointless."

"Did Fiona say why?"

"I suppose because she feared what the repercussions would be if she spoke out against him. He terrified her as well as intimidated her, or is that the same thing? Either way, give her a week or two, and she'll have forgotten all about him and will be able to live her life as it should be lived. Free from any kind of fear or intimidation."

"You seem pretty confident about that, Donna. Maybe there's more going on here than we've been able to uncover as yet. Care to fill us in?"

She cocked her head. "Meaning?" Then she wagged her finger. "Oh no you don't. Don't even go there."

"Go where?" Sam pushed, her heart racing.

"I can see it in your eyes. You're fishing, searching for clues that possibly one of us has done something bad to him. Seriously? And they wonder why most people don't trust the police. That's fucking tantamount to you telling me the abuser has more rights than the person he's abused."

Sam raised a hand to prevent Donna from saying anything that she was likely to regret. "We're not all bad, before you start telling me all coppers are either bent or couldn't give a toss about folk."

Donna gulped and held her head in shame. "I'm sorry if I've overstepped the mark. I'm lashing out because I'm gutted that Fiona has put up with years of abuse, and now that he's taken off, I can see where this is going to lead, to you blaming her for his disappearance. Am I right?"

Sam vehemently shook her head. "No, you're categorically wrong. All we're trying to ascertain are the facts, for now. What happens once we've collated all the facts? Well, there's no telling how that is going to pan out, not yet."

"I'm sorry. Maybe I'm guilty of doing you an injustice. The statistics are there for us all to see. The police are guilty of being totally negligent over the years, why should the general public trust you?"

"I can't speak for other officers on the force, all I know is that my team and I have never had a complaint against us, and we've solved virtually every crime we've investigated. There may have been one or two earlier crimes where we screwed up and let a suspect get away, but we've more than made up for our shortfalls over the years."

Donna nodded. "That's good to hear. Now you need to stop all this nonsense of thinking Fiona is behind *his* disappearance, because nothing could be further from the truth. For a start, my sister wouldn't have the brains to conjure up a scheme to get rid of him. No disrespect intended, and I would never voice my opinion in front of her or my mother. You need to look elsewhere."

"Okay, we'll go along with what you're saying, so tell me, where do we start searching for clues?"

Donna inhaled a large breath and sighed. "I don't know. Maybe you need to delve deeper into his finances. Last I heard he was doing the rounds with the family, trying to obtain at least ten grand. Is it possible he went to a loan shark and couldn't keep up the repayments? I might be talking bullshit, but it's got to be an avenue you need to follow up on."

"My team are dealing with that side of things as we speak, hopefully they'll have some news for us when we return to the station. Is there anything else you can think of that might have caused him to take off the way he has? Is it possible he might be having an affair with another woman, perhaps?"

"I'm not sure. Is that the sort of thing an abuser does? Or do they tend to concentrate all their efforts on ruining one person's life at a time? I'm totally out of my depth with that line of thinking."

"It takes all sorts to make a world, something we're going to look deep into in the coming days. What about places where he's likely to either hide or go to, any ideas?" Sam knew about his aunt's place in Torquay, but maybe Donna could give them more.

"You're asking the wrong person; that doesn't mean you should go back and hound my sister for the answers either."

Sam was getting irritated with her attitude. "We're not in the habit of *hounding* anyone, all we're trying to do is obtain the truth so we can form a picture to go forward. It's clear that something must have happened to have maybe tipped Rory over the edge on Sunday. A family day out led to him driving off and not returning home for the next two days. Does that add up to you?"

"No. Not at all. I've told you all I know. What I'm trying to say is that I did my very best to stay out of their marriage. We've all got our own shit to deal with in this life, haven't we?"

Sam cocked an eyebrow. "We have? Anything we need to know about, Donna?"

"Nope. I'm dealing with the issue in my spare time." She rose from her chair and marched towards the door. "Now, if you don't mind, I'm very busy. I'll show you out."

Sam and Bob followed her back into the spacious entrance hall. "Thank you for sparing the time to see us. Here's my card. If anything comes to mind that you believe would be of interest to us regarding the case, then please, get in touch," Sam said.

She took the card and slipped it into her coat pocket. "Thanks. I hope that bastard shows up soon. In my mind, he's doing this on purpose as another form of abuse for Fiona to have to contend with."

"We'll take your thoughts on board. Thank you for your time today."

"You're welcome."

Sam and Bob left the building, and they ran to the car through yet another torrential downpour. "Jesus, I reckon this weather has it in for us today. Every time we either arrive or depart from a location, we get caught," Sam complained.

"Moan, moan, moan, that's all you ever do, about the weather anyway. During the summer, it's either too hot and sticky or too cold in the winter, and now it's the rainy season, here we go again."

"Wow, don't hold back on my account, Bob. It's an English trait, talking about the weather, or had that fact escaped you?"

"Discussing it, yes, complaining about it... let's just say you could take it up as an Olympic sport."

"Sodding charming, that is. Anyway, putting the miserable day aside for now, what did you make of the interview with Donna?"

"To tell you the truth, it has only confused me all the more. Something doesn't add up, we just need to find out what that something is. Maybe she's right about the loan shark, they can be callous bastards when they need to be if someone doesn't keep up with their payments."

"But he drove away, that's what's getting to me. Without packing a bag or taking any of his belongings with him. If his intention was to take off, escape his debts, why the heck would he simply drive away? None of this is making sense to me."

"Maybe Alex will have something for us from the CCTV and ANPRs by the time we get back to base."

"Here's hoping. Come on, let's get back and have a cuppa to warm us up. Hey, I might even treat you to a sandwich en route."

"I'm up for that, not one to look a gift horse in the mouth."

"Do me a favour and call the station, see if anyone else on the team wants a sarnie. Might as well pick their lunch up on our way."

Laden with two paper bags full of sandwiches, Sam and Bob dished out the food, and the team gathered around to discuss the case.

Finishing her first mouthful, Sam asked, "Alex, any news of Rory's car on the cameras yet?"

He swallowed down what he was chewing and shook his head. "Not yet, boss. There's only a few in the immediate area, close to his home, nothing that you'd call right on his doorstep."

"Okay, keep expanding the search if you have to, he's got to show up on one of them soon. Claire, I don't suppose you've managed to get your hands on the bank statements yet, have you?"

Claire took a sip from her coffee and reached behind her. "Yep, I was going through them when you came in." She handed Sam the statements to glance through.

"Okay, he's overdrawn and accrues large amounts of interest every month from what I can tell. Over ten grand in debt, which adds up to what we've already gleaned from the interviews we've held so far. I'm going to put this out there: I think we should look into the wife being involved in his disappearance. I know all the arguments why we should avoid doing that, but there's just something not ringing true on this one. Everyone is telling us he abused Fiona, well, maybe now that she has Summer, her daughter, to be concerned about, perhaps she found an inner strength to put a stop to the abuse once and for all."

Bob kept tucking into his BLT, not even nodding his agreement to her statement.

"Bob clearly doesn't agree with me." She laughed.

"I'm too busy eating to think about anything else," he admitted, much to Sam's annoyance.

She let his comment slide. "I think our next step has to be me asking for the public's help. Someone must have seen the couple on Sunday. We need to form a genuine picture of events which took place that day. I'm reluctant to just take Fiona's word for what occurred."

"You really think she's behind his disappearance, don't you? With no evidence either way as yet," Bob challenged, his brow knitted.

"As I've said all along, there's something going on that I can't pinpoint that's making me twitchy. I'll get in touch with the press officer now, I refuse to get bogged down with going around in circles on day one of the investigation. A man has gone missing, someone out there must have seen him. Alex, you need to keep trying to track down his vehicle. I know that's a tough ask, but without that, we're up shit creek."

"I hear you, boss," Alex mumbled. "I'll do my best and go the extra mile." He raised what was left of his sandwich. "Once I've devoured my sarnie."

Sam finished her lunch while she studied the bank statement. "Nothing here, not really, apart from the ten grand in debt."

"Okay, hear me out on this gem," Bob said. "If we're thinking a loan shark is behind him going missing, surely there wouldn't still be a debt showing up on his bank accounts, would there?"

"Hmm... that's a fair point. If he'd borrowed a large sum then he would have placed the funds in his bank account to have wiped out the debt and to have stopped the interest accruing, wouldn't he?"

Bob nodded then took a sip from his cup. "Yes, any normal person in the same boat would do that. Very strange."

"Yep, too strange to fathom. We'll ponder on that in a moment. Let me get onto Jackie, see if she can magically summon up a slot with the media journalists for me, before the end of the day."

"It's pushing it, but if anyone can do that, it's Jackie," Bob added.

Sam nipped into her office to make the call. "Hi, Jackie, I'm in desperate need of your help."

"Hi, Sam, umm... isn't that always the case?"

"Oh yes, you're right. Silly me. Anyway, I'm hoping you can pull a few strings and get an appeal out before the end of my shift."

"I can do my best, I've got nothing else planned for this afternoon, so things are looking bright for you. What's the case?"

"A missing person. A man drooped his wife home after a day out and hasn't been seen since. His wife is desperate to hear from him," Sam added, which clearly wasn't true.

"I bet. How awful. Any sign of mental health issues? They're more prevalent since the lockdown."

Sam bashed her forehead. "I'm going to contact his doctor now, thanks for the reminder."

"Okay, I'll get back to you soon, hopefully with some good news."

"Cheers, Jackie."

Sam ended the call and then tried to call the surgery Fiona had mentioned her family belonged to. *Think, Sam, think! Ah yes, Moorgate Surgery. That was the one.* She smiled, pleased with herself, and looked up the number.

"Hello, Moorgate Surgery, how can I help?"

"Gosh, that was quick, I was expecting to be put in a queue." Sam chuckled.

"Can I help?" the receptionist repeated, unamused.

"Yes, I'd like to speak with the doctor who usually deals with Rory and Fiona Knox, please?"

"And you are?"

"Sorry, I should have introduced myself. I'm DI Sam Cobbs of the Cumbria Constabulary."

"We don't generally deal with requests such as this over the phone. Is it possible for you to drop by the surgery instead?"

"If I have to. Okay, I'll pop around and see you soon."

"Good. Thanks for your understanding. I'll get the patients' files out ready for when you arrive. Of course, I'll need to see your ID before I can get you in to see the doctor."

"Thanks, again. See you shortly." Sam hung up and debated whether she should shoot around there or wait by the phone for Jackie to get back to her. It took her all of five seconds to decide to visit the surgery first.

"Come on, Bob, we're off out. Claire, listen out for my phone, will you? Jackie Penrose will be ringing back soon, regarding a conference she's trying to pull together for this afternoon. Call me when she gives you a time. We shouldn't be long."

Claire nodded and raised a thumb in the air. "Will do, boss."

"Where are we off to now?" Bob complained in a whiny voice.

Sam shot down the stairs ahead of him and shouted over her shoulder, "To the doctor's. Got any ailments that need checking out while we're there?"

"Nope."

His abrupt tone made Sam pause mid-step and face him. "There is, isn't there? What's going on, Bob? A case of erectile dysfunction?"

"Sod off. You can be so full-on at times. None of your business," he added sharply.

"Hey, you do realise I was only teasing?"

"Whatever. Are we going to hang around on the stairs all day or get a move on?"

"The latter. You know where I am if you need to chat."

"I do, and it ain't going to happen. Thanks all the same."

Sam cringed, thinking she'd obviously hit a raw nerve. The drive to the surgery was undertaken in relative silence, apart from the sound of the radio filling the gap between them. Sam tried to apologise, but Bob grunted and stared out of the side window.

They entered the surgery, and the receptionist greeted them as frostily as she'd spoken to Sam on the phone. "Doctor Livesy is expecting you. Wait there a moment, please."

Sam paced the reception area until she returned to collect them. The woman opened the door to a room off to the right to reveal an older gentleman sitting at his desk with a stethoscope looped around his neck. "Come in. What can I do for you?"

"Hello, Doctor, thank you for seeing us. We'd like to ask you a few questions about Rory and Fiona Knox, if that's okay?"

"Yes, I have their files here. Take a seat."

Sam was surprised to see the old filing system in use instead of the doctor using his computer to access the couple's information. "First of all, I need to check if Fiona had an appointment to see you on Monday, with Summer."

"She did. Their daughter was running a bit of a temperature and had an upset tummy. Fiona seemed very agitated while she was here, clearly upset that her daughter was ill."

"I see. Thank you. Can I ask a few personal questions about Rory?"

"Within reason. Are you aware of the laws in place and what I have to adhere to?"

"I am. I'll ask tentative questions then with yes or no answers, how's that?"

He chuckled. "Nice try, Inspector. Go on, let's see how we get on."

"I have to say from the outset that we're here on official business.

Fiona reported her husband as a missing person, maybe that will help sway your decision slightly."

His eyebrows shot up. "I wasn't aware. Ask away."

"Has Rory ever come to you about any mental health issues he may have?"

The doctor searched his file and shook his head. "No, nothing like that."

"Ah, okay. Has he made any appointments to see you at all lately?"

"Not for around two years. Does that answer all your questions, Inspector?"

Defeated, Sam nodded. "Yes, unless you can give us any insight into his character?"

"I can't. I barely know the man."

"What about Fiona, can you tell us more about her? We're really struggling to make any sense of why this man just drove away from his family, Doctor Livesy."

"It does seem remarkably strange, but I can assure you, I see nothing in either of their notes that would make me think they were mentally unstable."

"Okay, let me tell you what we've discovered since our investigation began. Rory abuses his wife."

Doctor Livesy dropped the pen he was holding and sat back. "No. Now that has totally shocked me." He sat forward again and flicked through his notes once more. Then shook his head. "There is nothing in her files. No sign of abuse, no bruising and no mental trauma whatsoever. To say I'm flabbergasted would be an understatement."

"Several family members have told us, so it's looking like that's true. Okay, if there's nothing further you can tell us then we'll get out of your hair. Thank you for seeing us, Doctor. If Rory does pay you an unexpected visit in the next few days, will you ring me?" She slid a card across the desk.

"Of course, I will. I hope he surfaces soon. Maybe he just needed a break from family life for a few days. Having a baby around can sometimes come as a shock to the system for even the sanest of people, in my experience. No one is truly prepared how time-consuming parenting can be for a start."

"Hopefully, the truth will come out soon enough. Thank you again for your time, sir."

He stood, and they shook hands.

After leaving the surgery, Sam looked at her partner over the roof of the car and shook her head. "Is any of this making any sense to you?"

Bob shrugged. "I have to admit, no. There seems to be nothing cut and dried with this case."

They spent the rest of the afternoon back at the station, working with the team. At five, Sam held a press conference with journalists from the local TV station and several newspapers in the area. She was disappointed by the turnout but made the best of the exposure they had given her. During the appeal, she asked for anyone who had seen the family on their day out at Buttermere the previous Sunday to come forward. Knowing they wouldn't get any calls until later that evening, once the appeal had aired on the news, Sam insisted the team go home and get some rest. On the way out, she asked the desk sergeant to oversee the calls for the evening.

Her mind was a vortex of questions during her journey home. She entered the house to find Sonny in his usual spot, by the front door, wagging his tail profusely. She dipped her hand in her pocket and pulled out a treat. "You're a good boy. Give me two minutes and we'll go for a walk, okay?"

Sonny's wagging intensified, and he added an excited spin to the mix.

"Chris, where are you?"

Sam knew her husband was at home, having just passed the van in the drive.

"I'm up here."

Sam tentatively climbed the stairs, not liking the distant tone in his voice. She walked along the landing and found him in the bathroom, sitting on the toilet with his trousers still in place. Just sitting there. Puzzled, she asked, "Hey, what's going on?"

"Nothing, should there be?"

She pointed at the toilet. "Umm… don't try and tell me there's nothing wrong when you're sitting on the loo fully clothed."

"Damn. Okay, you've got me on that one. I'm contemplating."

She tilted her head and folded her arms. "About?"

"About what to do with the bathroom."

"Jesus, no. Not yet. Let's get through the winter first and decide in the spring what style we want to go with."

"Hey, there's no harm in looking. Planning things out."

"I'd rather you didn't, I haven't got over what happened with the kitchen yet. That was a catastrophe I'd rather not re-encounter anytime soon."

"I've learnt from that. You should be thankful I haven't stripped the bath out by now."

She raised a pointed finger. "You dare, Chris, and I'm warning you, I'll move out next time. Living in a mess for months with the kitchen tits up was enough to last me a lifetime, don't bloody put us through that again so soon."

He glared at her. "My take is that the sooner we get all the renos out of the way the better."

Sighing, she closed her eyes and shook her head to try to calm her flaring temper. When she opened them again, he was staring at her through narrowed eyes. She knew then that the battle was only just beginning. Instead of entering into a war of words, she turned and went into the main bedroom. Sam changed into a pair of jeans and a heavy jumper and went back downstairs to collect Sonny. After fastening a dog coat around the pooch's torso to protect his curly fur, she sorted through the coatrack and picked out her heavy waterproof jacket, slipped on her wellies and left the house.

3

At the end of the day, after being up against it at work, the last thing she needed was to enter a battle of wills with Chris. Once he'd set his mind on doing something, there was no going back. Sam knew she would need to dig deep into her resolve to remain calm when she returned. Chris had no idea how much his mindless actions were costing them financially. More than that, his dubious decision-making was taking a grave toll on their marriage. It was as if she didn't have a say in how things were going to turn out, despite the arguments that had ensued the last time he'd gone ahead and demolished their kitchen without putting the necessary plans into action.

I can't go through this again! Not again. Why does he keep doing this to me? Selfish pig! That's unfair, I know he's trying to make our lives better, but at what cost? Our bank balance is teetering on the edge of an abyss, and we haven't recovered from the trauma of the last time he had a good idea of what he wanted to achieve from the renovations. It's all getting on top of me.

"Hello, there. I was wondering if I would bump into you today. Are you all right, Sam?"

Bump being the operative word. "I'm so sorry, I didn't see you there, Rhys. How are you?" She peered out of her hood and searched the immediate area, looking for Sonny who she knew would be tearing around after Benji, Rhys's adorable golden Labrador.

"Hey, they're over here and they're fine. You're clearly not. Come, let's sit on the bench under the tree, at least we'll get a little shelter from this awful weather. The things we dog owners put ourselves through, eh?" His smile instantly warmed her heart.

"Yeah, it's not good, is it? Still, we don't complain about being out here getting a tan in the summer, do we? I suppose we have to take the rough with the smooth."

They moved over to the bench and took off their hoods. He had a piece of hair sticking up, and she had to resist the temptation to flatten it.

"A problem shared," he probed gently, ever the psychiatrist.

"I'm fine. A trying day at work, that's all."

He eyed her suspiciously. "Is that all? Are you sure?"

"Yes, I'm sure. How's your day been? Have you settled into your new offices now? Are you getting plenty of work?"

"Yes, all settled, which is just as well, the referrals are coming in thick and fast. I can see my days getting longer."

"Oh no, that won't be fair on Benji." She gasped and slapped a hand over her mouth then dropped it into her lap. "Sorry, I shouldn't have said that out loud."

He smiled. "Why not? I totally agree with you, which is why I've set up a doggie corner in my office. He'll be coming into work with me on a daily basis. If nothing else, it'll give me an excuse to take regular breaks to make sure he gets some exercise."

"Oh, that's so thoughtful of you. Benji is going to love being part of his dad's working day. I'm a little jealous now, wish I could take Sonny into work with me, I dread the thought of him being at home by himself all day."

"What about hubby, couldn't he take him to work with him?"

"He's tried it a few times, but told me Sonny drives him to distraction barking in the car all the time, so he's given up on him."

"What a shame. I suppose a doggie day care is an option, is it?"

"It would be if we had any spare cash. Hey, enough about me and my woes, the weather is gloomy enough without me throwing my dreary home life into the mix as well."

"I'm always here if you need to chat, you know that, right? Speaking as a friend, not professionally, of course."

"I know. But sometimes it's nice to come here and forget about what's going on at home. Does that make me sound heartless?"

"Not at all. Escaping a troubled marriage? Sorry, I shouldn't be presumptuous in thinking that."

"Why not? It's true. I've tried my best, but each day is filled with yet another argument, it's wearing me down."

He touched a hand to her cheek and whispered, "I can tell. I meant what I said, I'm a good listener. When you feel the need to offload, just shout."

"Thanks, it means a lot. This should be a fun place to come with the dogs, I don't want to blight the thought of coming here, does that make sense?"

"It does. You don't want to feel apprehension every time you come here because you associate this place as your escape haven."

She smiled. "Exactly. You're good." Sam blushed and averted her gaze from his intense stare. "The dogs seem to be having a blast. Sonny really loves his visits to the park to meet up with Benji."

"I'm with Sonny, except my desires belong with meeting up with his hooman."

They both laughed. The rain eased, and they decided to go for a stroll with the dogs down to the other end of the park, by the bridge over the pond. They chatted about their pasts and how involved they both were with their work.

"Does it cause conflict at home?" he asked out of the blue.

She smiled. "I thought we were going to avoid that particular subject."

He winced and groaned. "Yes, sorry, we were. Ignore me."

"No, it's fine. Chris doesn't really understand the passion I hold for my job. He's a landscape gardener, and although he takes pride in his work, he could up and leave it tomorrow and would never look back."

"Whereas with you, policing is coursing through your bloodstream, you view it as a vocation rather than a career."

She turned and applauded him. "Bravo, I've often described it that way myself. Do you feel the same about your job?"

"Yes, although years of intensive training have a lot to do with my way of thinking, too. Why would I give up on all those years if I didn't have it in my heart to carry on? I think I would feel physically sick if I ever decided to give it all up. Saying that, my parents would be devastated."

"Where do they live?"

"Up in Scotland, in Edinburgh."

"How wonderful. I plan on travelling around Scotland one of these years. Love the thought of being marooned on one of the islands, just me and Sonny."

He cocked an eyebrow. "You should go, it's a beautiful country."

"I know. I've visited Glasgow and Lockerbie before, but that's as far as I got. There are so many beautiful places in the British Isles for us to visit, not sure why people go abroad all the time."

"To escape. Life hundreds of miles away can heal people's souls, I suppose."

She cocked her eyebrow and looked around her at the mountains she could see in the distant landscape. "And places like this and our surrounding area can't?"

"Ah, you have a good argument there. But there are some of us who choose to take holidays abroad, to embark on the thrilling ride of jetting off on a plane to hotter climates."

"They're welcome to it. I'd much rather stay in this country to get my thrills. What do your parents do?"

"They're both retired now. Mum was a consultant and Dad a solicitor. Dad's a volunteer at the Citizens Advice Bureau now for a few days a week, just to keep his mind active, and Mum belongs to the Women's Institute and gets involved in all different types of charities with them."

"They sound like very caring people."

He smiled, and she could tell by the way his eyes lit up that his parents held a special place in his heart. "They are. They've always been there for me. A tremendous support throughout my career. What about your parents?"

"They're the best. Mum is a maths teacher, and Dad is a headmaster. I had a tough upbringing. When I say tough, it was filled with love, but they both pushed me academically, I have no regrets there. If it wasn't for them doing that, I doubt if I would be flourishing in my career today."

"That's great. They must be proud of your achievements."

"They are."

"Any brothers or sisters?"

She cringed. "One brother who I'd rather not discuss, and my sister, Crystal, runs a bridal shop in Workington."

"But you're close to her even though you don't speak to your brother?"

She sighed. "Yes, my sister is lovely. It's not that I don't speak to my brother, it's just that he let me down a few months ago and now he's being punished for his crime."

"Crime?" Rhys frowned. "Sorry, I don't mean to pry. I'm intrigued."

"All right, I'll tell you. It might do me some good, getting it out of my system. During a murder inquiry we were conducting a few months ago, I learned that my brother was caught robbing houses. He showed up at our place, expecting a handout; we were renovating our kitchen at the time and had no spare cash. He returned to the house and bashed Chris over the head, thinking we had money in the house. I was mortified when he confessed. It's hard to forgive a member of your family if they break the trust."

"How sad. Was Chris okay?"

"Yes, a bump on the head, that's all. I was horrified when I learnt that Mike was the one who had attacked Chris."

"So, is he banged up now?"

"Yep. Really, I don't want to talk about him. I feel let down that my brother thought attacking his family would get him out of the trouble he was in."

"What sort of trouble? Last question on the subject, I promise."

"Drugs. He's an addict going cold turkey in prison right now, I shouldn't wonder."

"Horrible to see someone sink to those depths to get out of a hole."

"Yep, he failed big time on all fronts."

The rain fell heavier around them. They trudged through the large puddles to find extra shelter beneath a couple of trees close to the exit of the park.

"I'd better be on my way soon, otherwise Chris is likely to come out searching for me."

"Is that truly on the cards?"

She laughed. "Nah, not in the slightest, he hates the rain. Only works in it when he's behind schedule."

"Can't say I blame him. It's nice to see you with a smile on your face now, despite the ghastly weather."

"Spoken like a caring psychiatrist. Thanks for listening, Rhys. Sorry if the conversation was a tad maudlin."

"It wasn't, believe me. Every time you open your mouth, I'm in awe of what's about to be revealed."

She chuckled. "Seriously? Have you seen a therapist yourself lately?"

"Nope, I don't believe in them. Shh… I didn't say that. Right, I'm going to leave you to it. See you again soon, and remember, keep your chin held high; the second it dips, a cloud darkens your features and covers that beautiful smile of yours." He leaned forward, kissed her on the cheek and walked away.

Sam remained there, frozen in time for a few moments, touching the heat on her cheek where his lips had just seared them. Sonny whined below her, breaking through her mesmerised state.

"Come on, handsome, let's get you home and dried off."

The walk home took place against a driving wind that had suddenly picked up. She entered the house, dripping water everywhere. After towelling the excess water off Sonny, she disrobed and ran up the stairs and jumped in the shower to warm herself up. From there she could hear Chris's faint shouts. He was complaining about the mess she'd left by the front door.

Sam dried her hair, pulled on her velour lounge suit and returned to find Chris sitting on the couch, watching TV. "Hey, you didn't tell me you were going to be on tonight."

"I'd forgotten all about it. What's for dinner?" she dared to ask.

"Ha, you tell me. I cooked last night, it's your turn tonight."

Avoiding another argument, she went into the kitchen and searched the fridge and cupboards, coming up blank at first until she put a list of ingredients into her phone and came up with a solution. *Pasta bake with chicken and chorizo, that'll do. Chris is bound to complain, but what the heck.* She spent the next ten minutes preparing the vegetables and cooking the pasta until it was al dente, then she combined all the ingredients and placed the casserole dish in the oven for thirty to forty minutes. She poured herself a glass of wine, sat on the bar-stool at the island and replayed the conference that had just aired on the news.

Chris entered the kitchen ten minutes later to see where his dinner was. "Not ready yet?"

"Does it look like it? If you were that hungry you could have made a start on dinner yourself. Oh wait, yes, I forgot, it was my turn to cook tonight."

"Wow, it was a simple question, Sam. You're pissing me off lately, snapping at me for no reason. Don't bother, I'll get something at the pub instead." He marched out of the room, and the front door slammed a few seconds later.

"Why? Why did I goad him? When am I going to learn to bite down on my tongue?" She looked down at the floor, and staring up at her was a confused Sonny, his head tilting from one side to the next. She bent to stroke him, and he jumped up onto her lap and slathered her in excited kisses. "Who could stay angry for long with you around? You're one precious dog, Sonny. I'm sorry to put you in this awkward position. Life will settle down soon enough. Not sure it will ever get back to normal, but we can live in hope, buddy, can't we?"

More kisses from her furry friend put a much-needed smile on her face. She popped Sonny on the floor and checked the oven. Her stomach rumbled as she opened the door and the aroma wafted past her. "Five more minutes and it should be ready to eat. Let's get your dinner sorted while I wait."

Sonny remained at her side until she placed his bowl containing a mixture of tinned food and biscuits on the floor. Pouring herself another glass of wine, she took her dinner into the lounge and flicked through the channels. Finally, she settled on a psychological movie she fancied watching on Netflix but it freaked her out after fifteen minutes. She switched it off and went to bed, alone, not for the first time lately.

4

Sam ensured she stayed out of Chris's way the following morning. He'd spent the night on the couch and was groaning in agony. *Good, serves you right for coming home in a drunken stupor, waking me up at bloody midnight. Selfish bugger!*

"I'm sorry," he mumbled.

She glanced up from her cereal and stared at him leaning against the doorframe like one of Count Dracula's latest victims risen from the dead. "Are you?"

"Yes. Can't we sort things out, Sam?"

"What's to sort out? If you want out of this marriage, you're going to have to search for the courage to tell me, Chris. I can't keep up the pretence that everything is hunky-dory between us, when it clearly isn't. I don't want this hassle in my life. We used to be happy together, I'm at a loss to know why you've fallen out of love with me."

He avoided eye contact and bit back defensively, "What are you talking about? I haven't."

"You could have fooled me. The way you've been treating me lately… well, oh, I don't know what to say any more. You need to sort yourself out, stop running away from the problem like you did last night. There are two of us in this marriage, not just me. And from what

I can remember, and what I've heard other people saying, marriage is a partnership, but you seem to have forgotten that."

His glare deepened. "You think you have the answers to everything, don't you?"

She let out an ironic laugh. "God, if only that was true. No, not in the slightest, but you know what? I'll die trying to be the best person I can be."

"And that barbed comment is supposed to condemn me?"

Once upon a time she adored looking at him, but just lately she had to swallow down the urge to hit him. "No, that's probably your guilty conscious pricking you again. I should be going. I have an important investigation on my hands and need to get cracking as early as possible on it."

"Work, work, work, that's all you ever think about. Well, that and Sonny. I come a lowly third on the list, I always have done, haven't I? Maybe I'm fed up with being at the bottom of the list of your priorities, instead of at the top."

"You're not, that's ridiculous you even thinking that's the case. I don't have time for this. We'll chat this evening, if you want to try to sort out what's wrong in our relationship."

"Whatever." He turned and stomped up the stairs.

Sam peered down to see Sonny staring up at her. She ruffled his head, and he whined a little. None of this was fair on him. Dogs picked up on bad feelings and awful atmospheres between their owners. She kneeled on the floor and gave him a hug. "Everything is going to be all right, I swear it will be. Hang in there. Now, go outside and have a wee before I leave."

Sonny trotted over to the back door. She let him out and looked up at the threatening sky while he did his business and then returned. "You're a good boy, Sonny." Sam threw a treat onto his bed and then got ready to leave. At the bottom of the stairs, she called up to Chris that she was going, but he ignored her.

On the way into work, Sam turned the music up loud, doing her very best to drown out the wayward thoughts about her doomed marriage filling her mind. It worked, too; however, she couldn't prevent the image of Rhys kissing her on the bridge at the park sneaking in there as well.

What a mess. What am I getting myself into? Am I being fair? What if there's no love left in my marriage? I'm tired of walking on eggshells at home. Tired of him turning his back on me and storming off like he did last night and this morning. I deserve better than that. We both do. Do I love him? I'm not sure any more. What about Rhys? What about him? I don't know how I feel. Yes, I do, who am I trying to kid? I'm flattered by the attention he's been giving me since I've known him, but am I prepared to give up my life as I know it, just to dive into another relationship so soon?

I don't know. I wish my fairy godmother would tap me on the shoulder and show me the path I should be taking.

The ever-cheerful Bob was standing by his car, tapping a message out on his mobile, when she pulled up alongside him in the station's car park. "Morning, you starting on that thing already?"

"Morning, not my fault if the missus insists on sending me a list of shopping to pick up on the way home this evening."

Sam chuckled. "Nice to see she's got you well trained."

"Hey, I like to think it's a great partnership we have. She gives me instructions, and I act upon them."

"You're an idiot. I'm glad you two have made it up, you deserve to be with each other."

He stopped walking and looked at her. "You sound a bit down, is everything all right at home?"

Sam batted his concern away with her gloved hand. "Never better. Come on, let's see what kind of response we received from the appeal last night."

"I wouldn't be holding my breath if I was you."

"We'll see."

They entered the building, and Nick, the desk sergeant, handed Sam a few dockets. "Thought you'd want to have these the minute you walked in so didn't bother running them upstairs and leaving them on your desk, ma'am."

"You couldn't be arsed, you mean," Bob corrected, earning himself a jab in the ribs from Sam.

"Uncalled for. Thanks, Nick. They seem interesting. All quiet overnight, case-wise?"

"Yep, from what I can tell."

"Good, that's what we like to hear, especially when we're already up against it with this particular one."

Sam punched her number into the security pad and entered the inner sanctum. Bob closed the door behind them. "Can't wait to see what's arisen. First, I need a caffeine injection to wake me up."

Bob tutted. "I'll get you one and bring it in."

"I don't care what Abigail says about you behind your back, you're an okay guy to me, Bob Jones."

"Yeah, that's about right, you women get the knives out when you're together. I'm surprised you haven't got a stash of voodoo dolls hidden under your beds to keep us fellas in line."

She faced him at the top of the stairs. "Damn, our secret is out."

"Funny."

"I do my best." She grinned and opened the door to the incident room. "Hey, Claire, what time did you get here?"

DS Owen glanced their way and smiled. "Not long. Scott needed the car as his is in the garage for a few repairs; he dropped me off on the way to one of his sites."

"Ah, that explains it. Busy, is he? Getting all the supplies he needs to carry out the renovations on his newly acquired properties?"

"Hit and miss. Some of his suppliers have been decent enough to keep some stock back for the regulars, at a cost, of course."

"Yeah, I can imagine. What, double?"

Claire nodded. "Sometimes even more than that. The building trade is in a shambles at the moment. We're lucky, though, so mustn't grumble. I can see so many trades going under if things don't sort themselves out soon."

"Must be an horrendous pressure on Scott's shoulders."

"It is. He's trying his best to remain upbeat about things that are totally out of his hands."

"It's all people in the building trade can do, I suppose. Send him my best wishes, tell him to hang in there."

"I will, thanks, boss."

"Now, would you like a coffee? Bob's offered to play waiter for the day, so be sure to take advantage."

Bob grumbled and crossed the room to the drinks' area. "I actually make quite a few. Not that you'd notice. White with one, isn't it, Claire?"

"Thanks, Bob. I'm impressed you remember after all this time."

"Jesus, don't you start on me." He returned with the three cups.

In the meantime, Sam had glanced through the notes and highlighted a couple of interest. "Okay, maybe, just maybe, running the appeal has proved beneficial this time around. I'll be in my office, chasing up a few curious leads."

Sam hadn't taken a couple of steps when the trill of her telephone ringing made her up her pace. She answered the call, "Hello, DI Cobbs."

"Sorry to trouble you so soon, ma'am, it's Nick on the front desk."

"I'm all ears, Nick. What's up?"

"You'll be pleased to know that one of my team has located the car registered to Rory Knox."

"Wow, that's fabulous news. Why don't you sound as excited as I am?"

"Umm... because of where it was found and the state it was in."

Sam's mood dipped instantly. "Go on. Give it to me."

"My lads discovered it out at the commercial estate on the far side of town."

"Okay, don't tell me it had been set on fire?"

"No, nothing as drastic as that. The door was open, and there's a large patch of blood on the front seat."

"Shit! Not what I wanted to hear first thing. Have SOCO been alerted?"

"Yes, they're en route."

"Thanks, Bob and I will get over there, see for ourselves. Get your lads to cordon off the area, will you?"

"Already instigated."

"Thanks, Nick. I guess I'll have to deal with the calls you handed me, later."

"Happy to oblige on both fronts, ma'am."

Sam hung up and raced back into the incident room. "You'd better bring your drink with you. They've found Rory's car."

"What? Where?"

"I don't have time. Come on, let's go."

In the end, they decided to leave their drinks behind and tore down the stairs at warp speed. At the bottom, Sam almost bumped into DCI Alan Armstrong.

"Morning, DI Cobbs. What's the rush?"

"Sorry, I don't have time to explain, sir. A man's life could be in imminent danger."

"Go. Make sure you fill me in later on today. You hear me?"

"I'll do my best, sir."

"You'll do more than that unless you want me to demote you."

Sam pushed through the security door and muttered, "Arsehole."

"That was uncalled for," Bob replied. "Oops, not you calling him a name, him telling you that you could get demoted in the first place."

"Yeah, ignore it, it's his way of keeping me in line. It gets on my tits, but what can I do about it?"

"Bloody report him. I would."

"Don't worry about it, Bob. I'm used to his idle threats. I'm the bigger person in our love-hate relationship."

"You're amazing. Such a strong woman."

"Ha... that's debatable at times. Come on, get in." They got in the car, and Sam immediately switched on the siren, if only to tick off the DCI. She knew he hated hearing the racket so close to the station. *Screw you, Armstrong!*

Bob laughed his socks off next to her. "He's going to pin you to the wall later."

"Yeah, possibly. But I'll take pride in the knowledge that I've pissed him off on the way down."

"You're killing me. Remind me never to get on the wrong side of you, I might not live to tell the tale."

Buoyed by the devilment pulsing through her veins, Sam weaved in and out of the traffic, out to the location. "Five minutes, must be some kind of record for us."

"Crap, I'm surprised I've got any nails left, some of them have snapped off."

It was Sam's turn to laugh. "What have I told you about spending your hard-earned money on useless manicures and extensions?"

"Sod off. Nothing could be further from the truth. I ain't into all that poncey stuff. I'm a *true* man."

She shook her head and sniggered until her throat became sore. "Have I told you lately how much you brighten my day?"

He grinned and pulled on the handle of the door. "Not enough."

They exited the car.

Sam's expression turned more serious. "Okay, back to work. Let's see what we've got. We'd better get suited and booted."

Bob scanned the area. "Why here? It's not like it's that remote, is it? There must be lorries coming and going around here at all hours of the day and night."

Sam passed him a protective suit and then stepped into hers. "I agree. It does seem strange. Maybe if someone has abducted him, they had another vehicle waiting and the whole thing took less than a few minutes."

"What about the blood?"

"I'm not sure. Let's hold back on the speculation for now and see what we're up against after we get a closer look at the crime scene."

Once they had changed into their suits, they made their way towards the uniformed officer holding the clipboard with the Crime Scene Log, and checked in. Then they dipped under the cordon and approached the two Scenes of Crime technicians, carrying out their respective tasks on the vehicle. One was busy photographing the possible crime scene while the other was taking swab samples from the inside of the car and the surrounding area.

"Hi, gents. What have we got here?" Sam peered over the shoulder of the tech who was taking the photos. He stood back to allow her to get closer.

"Stating the obvious, it's blood. We'll get it analysed. I'm presuming you have something for us to match the DNA to?"

"It can be arranged. I'll need to call round to see the wife anyway, to share the news after we've finished here. I can pick up something from the house and drop it over to the lab. Any idea how long we're going to have to wait for the results?"

"You do your bit and we'll get the results to you ASAP."

"Great news. How much is there? Half a pint?"

"Probably, yes. If you want my opinion, I wouldn't say it's enough for him to lose his life, but what do I know? He could have continued bleeding elsewhere."

"Any other clues nearby?" Sam's gaze darted around the immediate area, mainly searching the ground.

"More blood over here, near the road," the other tech called over.

Sam and Bob walked ten feet to join him.

The technician pointed out a couple of places on the ground. "Here and here."

"I see it. Less blood than in the car, only a few spots," Sam noted.

"Maybe someone pressed something over the wound. A dead hostage wouldn't be any use, would he?" Bob suggested.

"Fair assumption. We've got nothing else to go on right now." Sam peered through narrowed eyes into the distance at the nearby buildings. "Any chance there are cameras around?"

Bob followed her gaze and sighed. "Doesn't look like it to me. I can take a wander over, see if one of the units farther back has one."

"Yes, do it, Bob."

Her partner set off. Sam surveyed the area again, in more detail this time. "One road in and out of the area, right?"

"Seems that way. I know they're trying to obtain further planning permission for future developments."

"Interesting. That means whoever attacked the man, assuming that's his blood, must have come through the estate. The question is, why was he here in the first place? To meet someone? If so, why?"

"He might have been involved in a car chase and got trapped," one of the techs suggested.

"Another possibility for us to consider. Without any form of footage to back up our theories, we're screwed." Sam circled the car. "Any fingerprints?"

"Quite a few. Again, we'll need something with his prints on, and possibly his wife's, to rule her out."

"Hmm… okay. Is there any way of knowing if the wife was here with him?"

"Nope, not really. Not unless you find any footage to tell you either way."

"Frustrating."

"Do you have suspicions about the wife?" the tech holding the camera asked.

"Yes and no. It's there, in my gut and at the back of my mind. Of course, if I can gather evidence to the contrary, it will make life a lot easier all around."

"We'll do our best."

"I know you will." Her gaze was drawn to the road, at Bob making his way back to her. "Anything?"

"Yep, there's a camera outside one of the units a few doors down, but unfortunately it's locked up."

"Damn. We're going to need to get hold of the owner. Can you check it up on your phone, try to leave a message? Maybe the calls are being diverted to their home number or something."

"Already did that. No answer. I popped my head into the unit next door, and they told me the owner, a Frank Miller, was out for the day and due to return tomorrow."

"Great. I guess we have to be thankful he's not away on holiday, unavailable for a week or more."

"There is that. What do you want to do?" Bob asked.

"We'd better check if there are any other units with cameras. If we can't find any, I think we're going to have to call it a day here and visit Fiona. She needs to be made aware of what we've discovered. How far is their house from here? Why bring him here? With the intention to either kill him or abduct him?"

"We won't be able to answer that until we've viewed the footage, if there is any. Want me to ring the station, get Alex on the task of searching the ANPRs in the vicinity?"

"Good idea. It can't harm. Until we see what's going on with Rory's vehicle and what happened between him leaving home and possibly being followed here, things aren't going to make much sense to us, are they? Let's get out of this gear and back in the car, there's nothing more we can do here."

"Not as if there's likely to be witnesses around this area either. Where's an alert, or should I say, nosey dog walker, when you need one?"

Sam slapped his arm, his suit rustling under her touch. "Watch your mouth, you, I'm a dog walker, remember."

He grinned and set off back to the car. "Hush my mouth."

They disrobed, threw the suits into the boot and drove slowly back through the estate, passing all of the ten units which, disappointingly, proved that only one contained high-valued goods that warranted keeping safe with cameras. "How frustrating for us. Oh well, it is what it is. We'll time how long it takes us to get to Fiona's. Can you keep your eyes open for any possible cameras en route?"

"Yep, will do. Alex is going to ring us if he finds anything at his end."

Sam swallowed down the bile filling her mouth and knocked on the front door of the house. Fiona answered the door, cradling Summer in her arms. She stared at Sam and whispered, "Have you found him?"

"Can we come in out of the rain, Fiona?" Sam asked.

"Sorry, of course."

Sam and Bob entered the hallway and took off their damp coats rather than drip their way into the lounge.

"Please, I have to know if you've found him." Fiona lowered

Summer onto her knee as she sat in the easy chair. She motioned for Sam and Bob to sit on the sofa.

Sam watched the woman's every move intently, searching for possible signs of guilt. "We've just come from a location where your husband's car was found about an hour ago, Fiona."

Fiona gasped and hugged her daughter. "Is he all right?"

"I have to tell you that unfortunately Rory wasn't at the location."

"What? I don't understand."

"His car was found on an industrial estate, past some of the commercial units, on the wasteland beyond."

"His car? Not him?"

"Sadly, not. Umm… I've got some other news for you."

Fiona inclined her head and seemed puzzled. "Go on."

"We've had to call out SOCO to the scene as there was a large patch of blood found on the driver's seat."

Fiona gasped again and covered her mouth with her hand. Little Summer glanced up at her and started to cry. Fiona ran a soothing hand around her daughter's face and kissed the top of her head. "I'm sorry. Mummy's fine, Summer. Hush now."

The touching scene pulled at Sam's heartstrings. In that split second, she doubted her previous feelings about the woman. Was she guilty of doing her an injustice? "Are you all right? Can I get you a drink?"

"No. I'll be fine. I don't understand why there was blood in the car and yet Rory wasn't there. Are you telling me someone has hurt him and then taken him? Kidnapped him?"

"At the moment, until we investigate further, we're unable to say what exactly has happened to your husband. I take it no one has contacted you regarding his disappearance."

She shook her head and kissed her daughter on the cheek. "No, no one. What is going on? I can't believe this is happening to us. One minute he was here and, the next, he's gone. What am I supposed to think when you tell me his car has been found with a patch of blood in it? Where the hell is Rory?"

"Try and remain calm, it's only going to upset Summer."

She glared at Sam. "Don't tell me to remain calm. That's like a red rag to a bull in the circumstances. I demand to know what you're doing about his disappearance. People don't just vanish into thin air, do they?"

"We're doing our very best to determine what's happened to him. What I need from you is something with Rory's DNA on, either a toothbrush or a comb will suffice. Hopefully, we'll be able to match it to the blood we found at the scene."

"Goodness me. Okay, I've got that upstairs; as you know, he failed to take anything with him when he left. Do you think he was going to meet with someone and it turned nasty?" she asked, her tone less fraught.

"I suppose there could be a couple of scenarios we could be looking at. It's better not to speculate at this stage. Let's go with the evidence and try to work out what we're dealing with from that."

"I'll put Summer in her playpen and go upstairs." Fiona exited the room with her child and left the door open.

Bob leaned over and with one eye on the door, he whispered, "Have you changed your opinion on her yet?"

Sam shrugged. "I don't know. There's still something niggling me about this. Yes, she seemed shocked when I told her about the blood, but… I don't know, maybe it's me being too harsh on her."

"Possibly. She appears to be genuine enough to me. Sounds like the husband had a few dark secrets and that's what has got him in trouble. All she's guilty of is trying to process the information and struggling with it. That's maybe why you're having difficulty in believing her."

The stairs creaked. Sam and Bob halted their conversation and waited for Fiona to re-enter the room. Her eyes were red and her cheeks damp. "I'm sorry to be so long. I had to take time out to compose myself up there. It hit me hard once I put Summer in the other room. What do you think has happened to him? Here's his toothbrush and comb as requested."

Bob withdrew a plastic bag from his pocket, and Fiona slotted the items in and then retook her seat. Bob sealed the evidence bag.

Sam smiled. "I'm sorry. We're as much in the dark about this as you are. Did you see the news last night?"

"No. I made a point of staying away from the TV to play with Summer. She's missing her daddy."

"I see. Well, I made a plea to the public for help which aired last night. I have a few people I need to call back today who contacted the station after the appeal went out. With any luck, someone will have seen Rory in the past few days. Which might help us piece everything together. We have to hang on to the hope that he's still alive, Fiona."

"I'm trying, honestly I am, but it's so difficult not to fear the worst. I know he's not the easiest of people to get along with, but there's no reason on this earth why he should disappear the way he has. He wouldn't leave Summer for a start."

Sam cleared her throat and clenched her hands together. "We're aware of the abuse you've suffered, Fiona. You should have told us."

Her head dropped, and her gaze focussed on a worn patch in the carpet. "I'm sorry. Yes, I should have told you, it's very difficult for me to say the words. No one likes to admit they get seven bells knocked out of them, do they?"

"I suppose. How long has the abuse been going on?"

"Years. Too many to remember."

"Does he tell you why he strikes you?"

"Anger, frustration, his own inadequacies, jealousy sometimes, especially when he catches me talking to another man. At the end of the day, an abuser doesn't need an excuse to use their fists, they do it because it makes them feel better."

"I'm sorry you've had to contend with that over the years. Can I ask why you haven't reported it to the police before now?"

Fiona shrugged, and then her gaze drifted up to meet Sam's. "The police never believe the women involved. Most of whom live in fear every waking hour of their days. Once the abuse begins, it continues and rarely ends. I've done my research when I've been tempted to report it, but the statistics tell me there's no point in wasting police time."

"I'm devastated to hear you say that. Policies are changing all the time, people like you need to know you have our support. There are far too many abusive relationships in this country, we all need to do our best to stamp it out."

"Thank you. The truth is, living with an abusive partner can be a living hell, no place to hide from the abuse. The victim spends all their time walking on eggshells, waiting for the abuser's inner volcano to erupt. Still, you don't want to hear about that, it's not the issue here. My husband is missing, could be out there bleeding to death, and we're no further forward knowing why he left or what's happened to him. Why is that?"

"It's all going to take time to sort out, Fiona. We have a few leads we're keen to follow up on, but first, it was our duty to obtain the items you've kindly given us to match any DNA we found at the scene. I don't suppose you have the number for Mick, your husband's friend, do you?"

"I don't. He has all his personal numbers in his phone. I'm sorry for getting annoyed with you, I know it's not your fault. I'm conscious of the fact that I didn't notify you until yesterday as well. I guess, deep down, I'm feeling guilty about that."

"There's no need. You were thrust into a difficult situation, I can totally understand why you decided to drag your feet. Answer me this, has your husband ever harmed your child?"

"No, never."

"But it's always there, in your mind, that he might turn on Summer as she gets older, am I correct?"

"Yes, that's right. God, this is such a mess. Why didn't I have the courage to pack my bags and leave him years ago? If I had, neither of us would be in this predicament now."

Sam was puzzled by the woman's admission but should she be, given that Fiona had already informed her that he was an abuser? "Is there something you're not telling us, Fiona?"

"Like what? I admit at the beginning I hid what was truly going on but I've been honest and open with you here today."

"Okay, try not to get yourself too upset. I had to ask the question.

We're going to do our very best to find out what's going on with your husband; it's going to take time, though."

"Time? What if someone is holding a knife to his throat as we speak? Do you think that person is going to allow you the time it takes for you to solve this case? I doubt it. I don't know who has him, if anyone, or what is likely going on, all I know is that Rory left here on Sunday and I haven't seen him in the three days since. You tell me what I'm supposed to make of that?"

"Okay. The next step is for us to find out who the blood belongs to and go from there. We probably won't get the results back for another forty-eight hours or more. If you can be patient with us a while longer, I'd appreciate it."

"If I must. Will you let me know as soon as the results are back? What's going to happen to our car? Can I go and pick it up?"

"No. I'll let the SOCO team know that you're eager to get the car back, see if they can hurry along the analysis they need to carry out back at the lab. Again, we could be looking at forty-eight hours, maybe more with the vehicle."

"Okay, if there's nothing else you can do for me, I have to accept it."

Sam rose from her seat, and Bob followed. Fiona led the way to the front door, her shoulders slouched in resignation. Sam and Bob retrieved their coats and put them on.

Sam rubbed her arm. "Hang in there. We're doing our very best for you."

"Thank you. You have my number, please ring me if you hear anything."

"Either that or we'll come round and tell you in person."

She smiled, nodded and closed the door behind them.

"Jesus, that was tough. I hate having evidence at our disposal but no clues as to what has gone on. She has every right to be furious with us," Sam said on the way back to the car.

"I thought she handled it quite well, under the circumstances. I can understand her reluctance to ring us in the first place if he's used her as a punchbag over the years. Why the hell these women stay with these men is totally beyond me."

They entered the car before Sam replied, "You have to put yourself in her shoes, she has a baby to protect now. She couldn't just up and leave. Abusers usually control their victims, take away their bank accounts, any money they have. He probably stashed away her passport so she couldn't take off and escape his clutches. It's easy for an outsider to say she should have done this or that, but only the person existing in an abusive relationship truly knows the boundaries open to them. Women in her predicament feel helpless and unloved. Fear keeps them trapped in the home. Often their families aren't aware of the abuse, so they feel isolated and all alone."

"I get that. Makes me bloody sick. What gives a man the right to believe he can control a woman like that? You wouldn't put up with that shit, would you?"

"Nope, I'd knife Chris, if he ever laid a hand on me."

"Whoa! Really? You'd risk your career and your future freedom by lashing out?"

Sam shrugged. "The truth is, none of us know how we'd be likely to react in those sorts of circumstances. So who are we to judge someone living under those restrictions?"

"But what about the child? Surely the child would come first."

"I agree. I go back to the feelings I had at the beginning of the case, there's still an underlying feeling of distrust there. I can't explain it any better than that. If he's abused her for years, sorry, but who could blame her for killing him off?"

"Jesus, is that what you think?"

"No, but then again, I think it would be pretty remiss of us if we didn't regard her as a suspect. What if she's employed a hitman to get rid of him?"

"You said it yourself, abusers tend to leave their victims penniless, so how feasible is that notion really?"

Sam sighed. "True. I'm scrabbling around for possible motives. Let's get back to the station, there's nothing else we can do out here now."

"Shall we pick up a doughnut on the way?" Bob rubbed his slim stomach.

"I don't know how you manage to stay so slender with the amount of crap food you shove down your throat every day."

"I work out at the gym every other day, not to mention the bedroom activity Abigail and I indulge in weekly."

Sam held up a hand. "Stop. Too much information. Don't you dare say anything else on that front."

"What, going to the gym?" He chuckled.

"You're incorrigible. I'm glad you and Abigail have sorted out your differences."

"For now, until the next teenage drama rears its ugly head and drives another wedge between us. I envy you not having kids."

Sam fell silent, contemplating his words.

"Hello, I was expecting some form of barbed retort from you on that one."

"Not going to happen, Bob. You need to count your blessings, not everyone is able to have kids."

She saw him wince out of the corner of her eye. "Sorry, my size tens have done the business again, haven't they?"

"It's fine, don't worry about it." She turned the next corner and brushed a stray tear away.

"Shit!" he muttered.

She patted his hand. "Don't fret about it. Just ignore me."

"Fuck, I didn't mean to upset you. I'm sorry, Sam."

"You haven't. Sometimes it catches me unawares, that's all. I'll be as right as rain in a second or two. You worry too much."

"I wouldn't hurt you, not intentionally anyway," he said, his tone more serious.

"I know. Now, where's the best bakery you know around here?"

"The one closest to the station is just fine. If you pull up, I'll nip out, grab what we need and catch up with you back at base."

"That's a deal."

5

Once they returned to the station and had consumed their guilty pleasure of a wicked sugar-coated doughnut, Sam got on with the task she'd left hanging, getting back to the members of the public who had contacted the hotline.

Her first call was to a man who told her he and his friend had passed Rory, a woman and a child, up on one of the small hills in Buttermere, which backed up Fiona's account of what had happened.

Sam took it upon herself to call the café and speak to the owner, who also confirmed he remembered the family being there and that they appeared to have had an argument when Fiona spoke to someone at the next table. The family left not long after, the café owner recollected. Then Sam rang another caller who had travelled up to Honister Pass at the same time Fiona and Rory were up there. He told them that the couple had been close to the edge, at the very top, and Rory had his hand on Fiona's arm. The caller didn't think anything about it at the time, thought he'd witnessed a couple of sightseers who had got too close to the edge to take selfies. He hadn't felt there had been anything odd about what he'd witnessed, but doubts were now flooding his mind after seeing the news that Rory was missing. He was cut up about not informing the police sooner. Sam had reassured the man that contacting the station when he had was enough and not to worry any further.

She returned to the incident room to share the news.

Bob frowned, seemingly confused. "Shouldn't we send a patrol car up there, see what they can find? What if Fiona turned on him and pushed him over the edge?"

"I agree we should send a couple of men up there to look around, however, thinking about it, what would be the point? We have his vehicle back at the lab with a huge bloodstain on the front seat," Sam was quick to point out.

Bob sank back in his chair and placed his hands behind his neck. "Crap, I forgot about that. None of this is adding up, is it?"

Sam perched her backside on the desk closest to him. "Nope, none of it. Which is frustrating the hell out of me now. Claire, has anything showed up on the financial side of things?"

"I tried digging deeper, but no, nothing else has come to light. Only that he was ten grand in debt. Nothing worth mentioning in her account at all, bare minimum in there."

Sam shook her head. "We need to keep on top of things, mostly the CCTV and ANPRs, we need to know what happened to Rory after he left the industrial estate."

"And that's all we have right now to be going on with," Bob confirmed. "Which is nothing, not really. Even though a few people have rung in telling us they saw the family, there's nothing sinister in what they're telling us. I'll organise the patrol going up to Honister Pass, if you think it wouldn't hurt taking a gander. Maybe she drove the car back and later dumped it herself; saying that, it doesn't account for the blood."

"It's worth a shot! I'll start chasing up the lab for the results. They'll probably curse me, but this is an urgent case. Without some form of evidence for us to consider, well, we've got bugger all to investigate. Keep at it, guys." She went back into her office and rang the lab. The person she spoke to wasn't happy about being hassled for the results and promised Sam that he would get back to her as soon as the results were known. To combat her frustrations, Sam took it out on the paperwork that was piled high in her in-tray, the work she'd been avoiding for weeks now, then thought better of it and, instead she contacted the list of people Fiona had given her.

After an hour of frustrating calls, leading her nowhere, she decided to tackle the paperwork, whittling it down to a couple of tasks that would need further investigation on her part before she would be able to sign them off.

Mid-afternoon, she received a call that sent shockwaves through her system. "Hello, Fiona, how can I help? If you're ringing up to enquire if the results from the DNA are back yet, they're not."

She sniffled. "I'm not. Please, you have to help us. It's my mum…"

Sam's brow furrowed, and she dropped her pen and paid full attention to what Fiona was saying. "Take your time. What about your mother?"

"Dad has just called me, told me that she's been run over in town. What am I going to do? I can't lose her as well."

Sam's eyes bulged at the unexpected news. "All right, stay calm. Which hospital has she gone to?"

"Whitehaven. Dad's on his way over there. I want to go, but I haven't got a car."

"It's okay. I'll arrange a patrol car to come and pick you up. I'm on my way, I'll see you there."

"Thank you so much. I'll get a bag together with Summer's bits and pieces. I'm not leaving Mum's side. Apparently, she's in a pretty bad way."

"Okay, I'll organise things at my end. I know how hard this must be for you, on top of everything else you're having to deal with, but please, try to remain positive. I'll see you soon."

"Thank you, Inspector." Fiona ended the call.

Sam rang the desk sergeant straight away. "Nick, I need a car to go and pick up Fiona Knox, her mother has been taken to hospital and we've got her vehicle at the lab."

"I'll get on it right away, ma'am. Nothing serious, I hope?"

"She was knocked down in town, I believe. Thanks." Sam was about to hang up when Nick spoke again.

"Not the suspected hit-and-run?"

"What? I've got no idea. Fiona didn't mention anything along those lines. Have you got someone down there?"

"Yes, but it's the centre of town; the traffic, as you can imagine, is a bloody nightmare."

"Okay. Bob and I will go to the hospital. I'll get a couple of members of my team down there to see if they can help. They'll need to speak to any witnesses at the scene anyway."

"Thanks. I'll let my guys down there know."

Sam leapt out of her chair and grabbed her coat from the rack on the way through. "Bob, come with me. Fiona's Mum is in hospital. A hit-and-run incident from what I can tell. Alex, I need you and Liam to get to the scene to assist the uniformed officers, they're overwhelmed, trying to get things back to normal down there. Apparently, it's utter chaos. See if you can speak to any witnesses. Ring me when you can."

Alex and Liam slipped on their jackets and raced out of the incident room. Not long after, Sam and Bob followed them.

"Are you thinking this was intentional?" Bob asked. He clicked his seatbelt into place beside her.

"Too much of a coincidence not to. God, I hope Lynne's going to be all right, I fear for Fiona's sanity if she isn't."

"None of this is making any sense at all."

Sam and Bob drove to Whitehaven with the siren on and pulled up outside the Accident and Emergency Department around fifteen minutes later. She dumped the car on double yellow lines and they raced through the reception area.

"You can't park there," the young man behind the desk said.

Sam flashed her warrant card. "It's an emergency. The ambulances can still get by, I made sure of that."

"Okay. Don't say I didn't warn you. If you get towed away it'll be your fault."

"Fine. I need to know where Lynne Chanters is."

The disgruntled young man tapped a few keys and pointed down the corridor. "She's in triage at the moment. Go to the end of the hallway, one of the nursing staff will fill you in on what's going on when you arrive."

"Thanks for your help. I promise to shift the car as soon as possible, we need to find out how the patient is for now."

He nodded and issued a strained smile.

Sam and Bob raced the length of the hallway and came to a stop outside the triage department where an elderly gentleman was sitting. "Are you Lynne's husband?"

"Yes, I'm Phil, and you are?"

"DI Sam Cobbs and DS Bob Jones. Have you heard how Lynne is yet?"

"No. They're keeping me in the dark. Is there any way you can use your position to find out if there's any news yet?"

Sam smiled. "I'll see what I can do." She approached the door and knocked twice on it. The door swung open, almost knocking her off her feet.

"Yes?" a nurse in her fifties with her blonde hair tied back demanded.

"Sorry to trouble you. We're here to see if there's any news regarding Lynne Chanters. I'm DI Cobbs."

"Nothing yet. We're doing our best. Take a seat and allow us to do our job, Inspector. We'll let you know what's happening as soon as we're able to."

"Sorry, I didn't mean to interrupt."

The nurse closed the door again, and Sam reluctantly returned to the bank of orange seats. She sat next to Bob, opposite the distraught Phil. He had his elbows on his knees, holding his head in his hands.

"Why? Why her? She's usually so cautious crossing the road," he muttered, his voice breaking.

"Do you know what happened?" Sam asked.

"Not really. I received a call because we both had a bracelet made with each other's contact details engraved. Never, not in a million years, did I believe I would ever be contacted and told to come to the hospital because Lynne had been involved in an accident."

"Is that all you know about the incident?"

"Yes. I don't know much at all, just that a car knocked her down and left the scene. People tried to stop the driver, but he put his foot down and drove away at speed. Why? How callous can some people be? Isn't this family going through enough right now? To be here, in the hospital, how dreadful on top of Rory going missing."

"I know. It's hard to swallow. Fiona should be here soon. I've arranged for a patrol car to pick her up."

"Glad to hear it. It's a logistical nightmare, her not having a car. No one can rely on public transport, not when there's a baby in tow."

"I agree."

The clatter of heels rang out in the distance, and Sam looked up to see Fiona trotting up the corridor, pushing a pram.

"Is there any news?" she asked her father from a few feet away.

"Nothing yet. Thanks for coming, love. I'm sorry I had to call you. I didn't know who else to ring. I know Donna is interviewing staff today, she wouldn't want to be interrupted."

"What? Dad, you should have rung her, she's going to be livid when she finds out she's the last to know. Do you want me to call her?"

"Oh dear, yes, you're right. I never thought about the consequences. Yes, okay, she needs to be here in case anything happens to your mother."

"Dad, don't say that. We need to remain positive. Don't speculate, not until we've received more information from the doctor. Can you watch Summer for me while I call Donna?"

Phil smiled as she wheeled the pram towards him. "My pleasure. Hello, sweetheart, how's my favourite granddaughter doing today?"

Summer gurgled and laughed at Phil peering into the pram. Sam's heart lurched. She watched the tender scene, dealing with mixed emotions, and then glanced at her partner who was studying her reactions. She shrugged and smiled, trying to ignore the warmth touching her cheeks at being caught out.

Fiona rejoined the group. "She's on the way. She wasn't happy with being the last to hear of the news, so expect her to kick off when she arrives."

"Bloody marvellous. I hope she doesn't," Phil said. He pushed the pram back to Fiona. "How am I expected to think of everyone else, when my wife is lying here, severely injured?"

Fiona flung an arm around her father's shoulders. "Don't worry, Dad, she'll have cooled down by the time she gets here."

"I hope you're right. She's a moody cow at the best of times. Sorry, forgot myself for a moment there."

Sam smiled at him. "You don't have to apologise. Every family has its fair share of problems, I can assure you. Does anyone want a drink?"

"I'll have a tea," Phil replied.

"Me, too, if you don't mind. Here, I've got some change if you need it." Fiona pulled out a handful of coins, some silver mixed with oddments of copper.

Sam shook her head. "I'll get them, don't worry. Bob, can you give me a hand?"

Bob left his seat, and they went in search of the vending machine. "I think I spotted one near the entrance."

"Makes sense if that's the main waiting area." They rounded the next corner, and Sam pointed at the machine. "Two teas and two coffees. Damn, I didn't ask if they wanted sugar. I'll take a punt and put one in each, just in case."

They returned, and Sam handed over the drinks to Fiona and her father. "I take it no one has appeared yet?"

"No, no one. She must be in a bad way if they're still in there working on her," Fiona got close to Sam and muttered, clearly hoping her father wouldn't overhear.

"Try not to think about it. Let's keep an open mind for now."

Sam glanced up to see Donna heading their way.

Fiona groaned. "Here goes, I bet she kicks off. Look at the sour expression on her bloody face."

"Try not to goad her," Sam advised.

"What the hell is going on here? Why didn't you ring me as soon as you rang her, Dad? Why am I always the last to know about things like this, just because I'm the youngest, is that it?"

"Not here, Donna. Calm down, this is neither the time nor the place," her father reprimanded her.

Donna threw herself into one of the orange chairs farthest away from the rest of them. She crossed her arms and sank her chin into her chest. "Fine. Ignore me then. Don't know why I bloody bother at times."

"Don't be so childish. You're twenty-four, not fourteen," her father shouted.

"Typical. I'm twenty-five, Dad. Wrong again. She's always come first in your eyes. I bet you know her age without even having to think about it."

Fiona stood between the warring father and daughter and hissed at them, "Stop it. Now. Mum's in there fighting for her life for all we know, and you two are out here at each other's throat. Hasn't this family been through enough this week already?"

"Sorry," Donna's mumbled apology drowned out their father's.

"Me, too. Let's all be kind to each other. Don't regret our time together," Phil said, his eyes drawn to the door, willing someone in authority to emerge.

They all remained calm and quiet for what seemed a lifetime as they waited for news. Periodically, Sam and Bob took it in turns to pace the area. The longer the wait went on, the more anxious Sam became. She had experienced being at the hospital in similar situations before, when things hadn't worked out for the best. A sinking feeling had developed in the pit of her stomach. Eventually, a doctor appeared and broke the news to them.

"I'm so very sorry. We did our best, but it wasn't good enough. Your wife has passed away, sir."

Phil stared at the doctor and shook his head. Tears rolled down his pale cheeks. Fiona flung an arm around her father's shoulders and hugged him.

"What? How could this be allowed to happen?" Phil asked, his bottom lip trembling.

Fiona stood upright and took a step towards the doctor. "How could she die? It was just an accident."

"I'm sorry. The injuries she sustained were catastrophic. I assure you, we did our very best to stop the internal bleeding, but once the body decides to shut down the organs, there's very little we can do. We believe her spleen was ruptured. All the operating theatres were in use because of a pile-up on the motorway. She was due to have an emergency operation, but her body wasn't strong enough to continue the fight."

Donna sat there, her head still down, shaking her head. "Why? Can we see her?"

"I wouldn't advise it. She's covered in wounds and bruises. She suffered greatly at the scene from what I can gather. We did all we could to save her."

Fiona nodded. "We're not blaming you, Doctor. We're in shock, it's so hard to take in the information. She was our beautiful mother, the woman who protected us her whole life and now she's gone."

"I'm so sorry for your loss. I need to get back now." With that, he left the family to console each other.

Sam couldn't help thinking his manner was a little abrupt; maybe that was down to the death rates doctors had dealt with during the pandemic. Was every doctor the same now? Had their ability to talk to grieving relatives been hampered by the number of deaths they had encountered over the past couple of years? Was there any way back for the nursing staff under such circumstances? Such a strain on their shoulders throughout the pandemic, it must have affected them somehow. "We'd like to offer our sincere condolences. It wasn't the outcome either of us was expecting."

Fiona stared at Sam and shook her head as one by one, tear after tear dripped onto her cheeks. "Thank you. Can you find the person responsible for this? My mother was a gentle soul, she didn't deserve to die so young. She had so many plans she wanted to fulfil during her retirement, and now this. She's gone, no longer able to hold her grandchild. She loved Summer so much."

Sam rubbed Fiona's arm. "We're going to do our very best to find out who did this. You have my word."

"You should be out there, not here," Donna shouted, anger getting the better of her as she bounced to her feet.

Fiona tried to hug her sister, but Donna turned her back on her. "Donna, we're all feeling upset, don't start mouthing off like you usually do."

Donna faced Fiona and squared up to her. "Mouthing off? You've got a bloody nerve, Miss Drama Queen twenty twenty-two. Oh, yes, that's right, everything is about you and that damn kid of yours, isn't it? No one else's feelings matter, do they? Well, I have news for you, she was my mother as well, in case you hadn't realised." She walked towards the wall and rested her forehead against it, sobbing, her shoulders jiggling.

Fiona and her father stared at each other, appearing to be helpless. Until her father shrugged and moved to comfort his youngest daughter. "Don't do this, Donna, not here, not right now. I've lost my wife, you girls have lost your mother, don't say something you're likely to regret when all the pain and grief subsides. Tensions are fraught at this moment. Let the situation run its course without getting into an argument with either of us, please. I'm begging you."

Donna launched herself off the wall and into her father's waiting arms. "I'm sorry, Dad. I didn't mean to lash out. I can't believe she's gone."

Fiona joined them in a family hug. Sam realised it was time for them to leave. She and Bob slipped away quietly.

"Damn, that was tragic," Bob muttered on their journey back through the busy hospital. They arrived at the exit to find it teeming down with rain.

"Bloody hell, can this day get any gloomier?"

"I know, pain in the arse. Want to make a run for it?"

"We're going to have to, can't stand around here all day." Keys in hand, Sam legged it for the car and jumped behind the steering wheel.

"That's it, we're going to be wet through for the rest of the day now." Bob groaned.

"I hate to tell you this, but we've got to drop by the crime scene now. I want to see for myself how this happened."

"Great. I don't suppose you've got an umbrella lurking in that boot of yours, have you?"

"I think I have, somewhere. I can't guarantee what state it'll be in, though." She started the engine and set off, relieved that the car hadn't been towed away for being illegally parked during their time with the family.

6

*A*lex and Liam resembled drowned rats at the scene when they arrived. They seemed surprised to see Sam as she and Bob approached them.

"What is it with you men? Why don't you ever use an umbrella?"

Alex shrugged. "Two reasons, one because I don't happen to possess one."

"And the other?" Sam asked, sensing she shouldn't have bothered by the glint in her colleague's eye.

"I wouldn't be seen dead holding one, it's hardly image-enhancing, is it?"

"Image-enhancing? You're hopeless, Alex Dougall. What have we got, anything useful?"

Back in efficient copper mode, Alex pointed at one or two people in the crowd standing under the canopy of a few of the nearby buildings, doing an excellent job of sheltering them from the soggy elements. "A couple of witnesses. Both saying the same thing."

"Which is?" Sam probed.

"The victim got off the bus and went to walk across the road, which was relatively clear at the time, what with the lights changing. When out of nowhere, this car came blazing towards her. The woman stopped in the middle of the road, appeared to be glued to the spot, unable to dive for cover. One man said she seemed mesmerised. I'm thinking she knew who the driver was, got a good look at him before the car struck her."

Sam surveyed the area in front of her and then she lifted the umbrella to peer over her shoulder. "Ouch! Not so good. Which direction did the car come from?"

"Over from the right. The lights had changed here. One bloke said he thought he saw the car parked up and move out of a space, while another man said the car flew at the woman, but he thought it was waiting at the lights."

"Either way, sounds like some pretty severe inaccuracies we can do without," Sam admitted with a groan.

"I know, very annoying, boss," Alex agreed. "We've taken the statements down from the two men, but we're also asking the rest of the crowd if they saw anything and getting nowhere fast."

"Bloody rubberneckers," Bob said through gritted teeth. "You'd think they'd have something better to do with their time on a foul day such as this."

"Human nature, it's the pits at times." Sam lowered her voice and gestured for Alex and Liam to lean in to listen to what she had to say. "The woman died. Her injuries were far too severe for the doctors to save her."

Alex struck his thigh with a clenched fist and shook his head. "Fuck, I had a bad feeling that was going to be the case once the witnesses described how fast the car was travelling, and the fact the driver didn't stay around to face the music. Do you think this was intentional, boss?"

"It's seeming more and more like it to me." She glanced around at the buildings. "You know what I'm going to say next. Any CCTV footage we can find is going to be a bonus. That should be our next step, to seek that out."

"Already on the case, boss. The laundrette opposite and the TV repair shop both have CCTV. I've told them to make a copy of the incident and I'll return to pick it up later."

"Good man. Why don't you chase those up now and then get back to the station to dry off? Bob and I will question the witnesses again and see if anyone else can throw in their tuppence worth. We shouldn't be long behind you."

Alex and Liam both nodded and marched towards the laundrette and the repair shop. Sam and Bob chatted for a while until they emerged holding a disc each.

"This is a bit off-the-wall, but hear me out, boss," Bob began, his gaze glued to the blood patch in the middle of the road that the rain was doing its best to wash away. "You don't think there's a connection, do you?"

"Between Rory going missing and Fiona's mother getting killed? I'd say that was an absolute certainty. But there are so many questions we need to seek the answers to."

"Such as?"

Sam chewed on the inside of her cheek as she contemplated the answer. "The main one for me is, why the hell hasn't the person who abducted Rory contacted the family, or Fiona, to make any demands? What's that all about?"

"Fucked if I know," Bob mumbled. After a few seconds thinking time, he asked, "What if the kidnapper is forcing Fiona to do something against her will, before they release him?"

"Like what? If that's the case, why kill her mother?"

"To get the point across. Hey, do I have to remind you that you've had an unexplainable feeling about this case from the word go?"

Sam sighed. "No, you don't. You might be right, the kidnapper might be forcing Fiona to take him seriously now."

"I reckon. Maybe she wasn't prepared to bow down to the kidnapper's demands because of her internal dislike for her husband, you know, what with him abusing her for years, so the kidnapper hatched a plan to make her take him more seriously, by killing her mother."

Sam stared at Bob and reluctantly nodded. "Possibly. Is the killer about to strike again?"

"Only time will tell. Where do we go from here?"

"Let's see what else we can glean from the onlookers first before we head back to the station."

Over an hour later, after Sam had asked the same question over and over to the crowd, they drove back to base, feeling more than a little dissatisfied. Sam fixed herself a coffee and asked Alex to show them the footage he and Liam had collected from the two shops. The scene was horrendous to watch. It was obvious the attack had been intentional by the way the driver put his foot down the moment he had Lynne Chanters in his sight. The woman was cast aside by the vehicle. It was evident that she wouldn't have stood a chance of surviving the accident, and Sam realised it was a miracle Lynne had clung on at the hospital for the length of time she had.

Feeling physically sick by what she'd witnessed, Sam made her excuses and nipped to the ladies' where she dabbed cold water on her face. *How could they? Who are you, you fucker? To deliberately set out to destroy this family. Why not be content with holding Rory hostage? Why go after Fiona's mother? Not with the intent to kidnap her but with one aim in mind, to kill her? Because Fiona isn't jumping through hoops for the kidnapper/killer? What does he or she expect from her? She's a mere housewife. No access to a bank vault to rob, nothing of that nature, so why hold a member of her family hostage? Maybe Rory has already been killed, and it's just a matter of us now trying to find his body.*

Sam returned to the incident room to find DCI Armstrong waiting to see her. She flattened her hair and tucked in her blouse under his scrutinising gaze.

"A moment of your time, Inspector Cobbs, in your office." He marched ahead of her.

Sam made the sign of the cross to her partner and trotted after him, leaving Bob to instruct the rest of the team. She followed the DCI into the office to meet her fate.

Armstrong sat in the visitor's chair beside the desk, allowing Sam to stroll past the window and get comfortable in her own chair. "To what do I owe the pleasure, sir?"

"Don't go getting your hand up your arse, I thought I'd drop by to see how you're getting on with the abduction case. I saw the appeal go out; anything obtained from that worth mentioning?"

"Not really. We had a couple of walkers confirm the family were in Buttermere and together up the top of Honister Pass on Sunday."

"And yet the man is still missing."

Sam nodded and sighed. "I should tell you what else has been going on. Please don't blame me for not bringing you up to date, it's been a tad hectic around here the last few days, to say the least."

"You seem stressed. Why don't you tell me what you've got so far and I'll see if I can help?"

Sam shrugged. "In a nutshell, we've got Rory Knox who has been abducted, so we believe, although his car was later recovered with a large patch of blood on the driver's seat."

"Is it his?"

"We're awaiting the results of the DNA analysis."

"And when should that be on your desk?"

"Within a day or two; they're doing their best for us, so I don't think I need to pile on the pressure anytime soon."

"Good, good. And what if the results come back not as expected?"

"Then we're up the creek. Even if they do come back as a positive result, we're still not going to be any the wiser. The amount of blood found at the scene could indicate that we're too late and Rory has already lost his life."

"So you would need to switch the investigation to a murder case instead. Is the wife anxious? Being cooperative? Could she be involved in his disappearance?"

"All of the above, it's a tough one to call. In all honesty, the pendulum keeps swinging one way and then the other with me wondering whether she's involved or not. Saying that, what occurred today has kind of turned the investigation upside down."

He tilted his head. "What's that?"

"Fiona's mother was killed in a hit-and-run. Not at the site, she died later at the hospital. Bob and I were there at the hospital when the doctor broke the news to the husband and his two daughters."

Armstrong tutted. "Jesus! That's dreadful, and you think there's a connection between the two crimes?"

"Don't you? There has to be, I don't believe in coincidences."

"What's your next step?"

"We're going to go over the footage from the 'accident', see what clues we can pick up from that. I'll keep on top of the lab, without putting pressure on them. My team are still going through the family's background. Nothing has shown up in the bank statements, only that Rory was ten grand in debt. After speaking to the family, we gleaned from his statement that he had asked around, trying to borrow the money, but no one had any spare cash to get him out of a hole."

"What does that lead you to believe?"

"We could be looking at a case of him obtaining the money from a loan shark, who is possibly now using aggressive tactics to get the money back. That's the only probability I've managed to come up with so far. Not good, I know, but the evidence is severely lacking on this one, sir. I'm open to suggestions if you can think of any."

He shook his head and rose from his chair. "Sorry, to me you have everything covered. Just keep me informed."

"I will. Thanks, sir."

He left the office, and Sam inhaled deeply then let the air escape again. She rotated her head to relieve the tension in her neck and returned to the team. "Right, well, that has wasted around thirty minutes of my time. What have you discovered in my absence?"

Bob lined up the recording and paused it several times. "Here, we've got a partial on the plate; further on we can see the full plate on the other disc. I've put an alert out on the car."

"That's excellent news. What about the driver? Any images of him?"

"Nope. We've caught a glimpse of a vague side view in one of the cameras, but because of the speed of the vehicle, the image is very blurry," Bob said, his tone one of disappointment.

"Stick with it, guys." Sam left the team doing their best to search for any evidence likely to break the case wide open and settled in her office for the rest of the day. Late afternoon, she called the lab, but was given the brush-off and told it was far too early for any results and to stop badgering them.

At six-thirty, Sam called a halt to their day. "You've done well today, folks. Let's see what tomorrow brings to the table. Have a good evening."

Bob waited for the rest of the team to leave and perched on the desk closest to the door. "Still frustrated?"

"And some. The DCI was hopeless offering me any solutions suggestions. He was just as perplexed by things as we are. Someone, somewhere, knows something. I can't help wondering if we're missing something obvious, Bob. What's your take on things? Go on, be honest."

He exhaled a large breath. "I feel the same way you do. Hopefully, now we've got a plate number for the car that mowed down Lynne today, it will at least lead us to the culprit."

She shook her head. "See, that's where the doubts are clouding my mind, it seems too easy. If the intent was there, wouldn't the culprit have removed the plates on the car to avoid being captured?" She pointed at her partner. "I bet you a tenner the car is found abandoned tomorrow."

Bob rose from the desk and switched off the lights. Sam followed him out of the room. "I have no intention of shaking your hand on that one because I think you'll probably be right."

"What about tracing the car through the ANPRs, were you able to discover which route it took to and from the scene?"

"Yep, sort of. We watched it leave the area and dart down one of the nearby side roads, it was as if the killer knew he'd be picked up by the ANPRs on the other major routes in the area."

"A wise killer, methodical, well-organised, not a chancer?"

"Sums it up, I'd say. Either way, he escaped the busy thoroughfare and has left us high and dry, searching for clues."

They waved farewell to the evening desk sergeant and left the station. "Maybe looking over the evidence again in the morning, with fresh eyes, might reveal something we've missed."

"We can live in hope. Have a good evening, boss."

"You, too. Say hi to Abigail for me."

Bob smiled and slipped into his car. Sam dropped into her driver's seat and drove home on autopilot, her eyes tired from the glare of the headlights coming towards her on the main road out of Workington. When she arrived home, Sonny was there to greet her with his tail wagging and his front feet dancing. "What do you want, mister? As if I didn't know."

Without changing her shoes, she unhooked his lead from the coatrack. They left the house and walked towards the park.

"Hello, you. I was hoping I would bump into you today."

A flutter surrounded her heart at the sound of his unmistakable voice. "Hello, Rhys. Oh, why were you hoping to see me?"

"Because when I see you, you brighten my day. Let's face it, today has been pretty dire weatherwise. How has your day been?"

"Nothing much to write home about, not really. Another murder inquiry to pass away the day."

"Oh dear. Well, I have to say, I wasn't expecting you to say that."

They talked and walked the length of the park and back, ignoring the fact that it had started to rain slightly in fits and spurts. Being with Rhys meant nothing dreary happened in her life. Or was that her imagination?

"Fancy going for a drink?"

"I should get back home," Sam replied, disheartened.

His smile never wavered. "I understand. Maybe another time, soon."

"I'd love to."

They parted at the exit to the park. He kissed her gently on the cheek again, taking her breath away, and drifted off. Her heart went with him. Sam walked home in a virtual daze to find the house still empty. After feeding Sonny, she opened the fridge to see what she could knock up for her own dinner, only to find it lacking in ingredients. As a last resort, she opened a tin of tomato soup and heated it up. While she ate her meal at the table, her thoughts turned to her relationship with Chris. Where was he? Silly question, she already knew the answer to that. He was bound to be at the pub, as usual. It didn't matter to him that Sonny had been left alone all day, why should it? He was her dog, after all.

Sighing, she cleared up and went upstairs, Sonny close to her heels. Sam showered and got into bed, picked up her Kindle and read until her eyes drooped. Giving in, she switched off the light, noting that it was already ten-thirty and no sign of Chris yet. She was tempted to go back downstairs to put the latch on the door, but she knew that would only make things a hundred times worse when he eventually staggered home.

Surprisingly, she managed to drift off to sleep, despite winding herself up about Chris's drinking.

A loud noise woke her at around midnight. Sonny growled from his bed by the door. "It's okay, Sonny. Go back to sleep." She slipped on her robe and went to the top of the stairs. There, she saw Chris leaning against the rack, trying to remove his coat and laughing at his own antics. Disgust welled up inside her. *How can anyone get into such a state? Why? Time and time again he does it, why? It's not like we're rolling in it at the moment. He knows how short of cash we are and yet he's still prepared to go out every other night and get pissed. Should I be grateful it's not every night?*

She turned on the hall light, startling him. He glanced up, swayed and lost his footing, falling headfirst onto the stairs.

"Oops!" he said; even that one word came out slurred.

The disgust soon turned to anger which made her retreat into the bedroom. *He can sort himself out, I'm not going down there to help him. Maybe that makes me out to be as selfish as him, so what?*

Sam climbed back into bed and pulled the quilt over her head to block out any further noise.

The alarm woke her at seven the following morning. She felt the bed beside her—it was empty. Slipping out from under the covers, she walked to the top of the stairs only to find Chris in the same position, snoring. *What the fuck? How could anyone sleep like that? I suppose if you're drunk enough, you'll sleep anywhere.*

"Chris. Chris, are you awake?" she asked in her normal voice. When there was no response from him, she asked again, this time three times louder.

He groaned and lifted his head, turning it from left to right. "What the... where am I?"

"You slept on the damn stairs," she bellowed, not caring if she hurt his head or not.

He glanced up at her, shielding his eyes from the glare of the hall light just behind her. "What? I couldn't have done."

"Look around you. You did." She'd said what she had to say and marched back into the bedroom. She patted Sonny on the head before jumping into the shower to begin her morning routine. When she emerged, she found Chris sitting on the bottom of the bed, waiting for her.

"I'm sorry, Sam."

She avoided eye contact with him; instead, she opened her wardrobe and sorted through her clothes. The red blouse caught her attention, it was the same one she'd worn the first time Rhys had kissed her. She did her best to push the memory aside, but failed.

"Don't ignore me, Sam."

Her fist clenched around the trouser suit she'd extracted, and she gritted her teeth, fearing what she might say if he pushed her too far. No, it was best for both of them if she remained quiet.

Only Chris refused to let things lie. He stumbled across the floor, clearly still feeling the effects of last night's boozy encounter, and grabbed her arm, forcing her to face him. "I said don't ignore me."

"Why shouldn't I? Considering the bloody state you're in. I didn't sign up for this, Chris." *There, I've said it. Make of that what you will!*

He had the decency to look ashamed. "I know, neither did I. I fancied a pint, that was my intention, to just have the one and come home."

"Ah, right, but your mates twisted your arm and you couldn't say no, is that it?"

He nodded. "Yes. These things happen. Give me a break, Sam."

"I left you alone last night, I gave you a break then. I don't have time for this, I'm in the middle of an important investigation."

He spun around quickly and lost his balance. He landed on top of Sonny, who yelped. Sam flew at him, yanked him by the arm, shoved him aside and checked how Sonny was. "Are you all right, baby boy?"

Sonny whimpered and held up his front paw. She clasped it gently, feeling for any broken bones. Sonny licked his paw, and then his tongue lashed her face as if telling her it hurt, but he was all right. She kissed him on the head and jumped to her feet. "What the hell is wrong with you? To be in this state at this time of day. You know what, I've had as much as I can take of this. Pack a bag and get out of my sight for a few days."

"What? I'm not going anywhere."

"Either you move out or I do, and as it's my money paying the mortgage and our debts at the moment, the logical answer would be for you to go, not me."

"Bollocks. I pay my fair share of bills around here."

"When you're not spending your money down the pub, you mean? When was the last time you gave me any money to stock up the fridge or the kitchen cupboards? You think the food magically appears there by itself or that the fridge fairies drop by during the night to replenish the stock? Get a life, Chris."

He ran a hand through his hair, as if the consequences of his drinking had finally hit home. "I'm sorry. I'll do better, I promise."

"Will you? This isn't the first time we've had this conversation, and I doubt if it's going to be the last either, not until you promise to get your act together and stop spending money we can't afford to waste. Sorry if you think I'm being unreasonable. I happen to believe keeping a roof over our heads is far more important than giving our hard-earned money to the landlord of our local. Wasting hundreds of pounds a week we just don't have. Where do you draw the line, Chris?"

His chest inflated. But he didn't have the words to counter what she had laid out before him. Instead, he turned his back and walked out of the room.

Sam exhaled and stared down at Sonny who was looking desperately sorry for himself. She knelt beside him and gently stroked his injured paw. This time he snatched it away from her and whimpered. "Great, now I'll have to take you to the vet's. I'm sorry, boy, you don't deserve to get caught up in this. Whatever *this* might be." *How the hell am I going to get you to the vet's today with me up against it at work? I can't rely on Chris to take you.* Sam saw her phone on the cabinet and rushed to pick it up. She punched in a number and waited for her mother to answer.

"Sam, is that you?"

"Damn, did I wake you, Mum? I'm so sorry. I forgot what time it was."

"My alarm is due to go off soon, don't worry about it. Is there anything wrong?"

"Umm… I need to take Sonny to the vet's and I'm up against it at work. I wondered if you could take him for me. Don't worry if you're busy."

"Oh no. What happened?"

"A silly accident. Chris didn't see Sonny lying in his bed and fell on him during the night on the way to the bathroom. I've just checked him over and I think his paw is hurt."

"Oh my, how clumsy of Chris. Can't he take him?"

"No, he's behind schedule on a job, and the building inspector is due today." Sam cringed as the lie tripped out of her mouth, which galled her. She'd never knowingly lied to either of her parents before.

"Very well. I have a couple of free periods after lunchtime, so if you can make the appointment around twoish, that would suit me."

"I won't be able to ring until nine. I'll get back to you after that. And thanks, Mum. I really appreciate it."

"No problem. Give the wee man a hug from me."

"I will. Speak later." Sam hung up and then squeezed Sonny. "That's from Grandma, she'll take you to the vet's later, we'll get you sorted, sweetie." A sudden thought struck her, that there would be no trip to the park after work that evening if the vet found anything seriously wrong with Sonny.

Ignoring the gloominess of the situation, she finished getting dressed and then ventured downstairs to enter round two with Chris. He was sitting at the kitchen table, his hands clenched around a mug of coffee.

"The kettle has boiled if you want a cup," he murmured.

"Thanks. Just to let you know, I'm going to try and book an appointment at the vet's for today. You injured Sonny when you fell on him."

"Shit! Are you sure? I'm sorry, it wasn't intentional."

"It never is, is it? When are you going to realise your actions always have consequences?"

"Don't start again, Sam. I've had enough for one day."

"In other words, you're too hungover to deal with it."

"Whatever. Get off my back, you've made your point."

Sam shook her head in disgust. She poured herself a coffee and slung a piece of bread in the toaster, not knowing if she'd be able to stomach it when it was ready, then she ran upstairs to get Sonny. She lifted him gingerly from his bed and hoisted him in her arms and, securing her treasured furry friend against her chest, she descended the stairs. Chris was waiting at the bottom with the front door open.

"There's no point asking you if you can manage, you're Super-woman and you'll probably end up biting my head off again."

"Just go to work. Get out of my hair, Chris."

He slammed the door behind him. Sonny jumped and whimpered in her arms. She gave him a comforting squeeze and then carried him through the kitchen and out of the back door to relieve himself. She lowered him to the ground gently. He hobbled around a little and crouched to do a wee rather than cock his leg. "You poor baby."

Sam picked him up again, carried him inside and placed him on the bed she kept for him in the kitchen. She pampered him with a few treats and set a fresh bowl of water and food by his side. "I hate to do this, but I've got to go to work, Sonny. Grandma will be around to see you later."

Sonny rested his head on his good paw and stared at her. His sorrowful eyes pulled at her heartstrings. She turned her back before the tears fell, detesting herself for leaving him in his hour of need.

7

Sam arrived late for work, held up by an accident caused by yet another unwelcome downpour overnight. Her first chore was to call the vet's at nine. The number was engaged a couple of times before it successfully rang on her third attempt. "Hi, I was wondering if you have an appointment for this afternoon, please, for my dog, Sonny, who seems to have hurt his paw."

"Let me have a look. What about two-fifteen, how's that?"

"Excellent. I'm at work all day, but my mother will be bringing him in, I hope that's okay?"

"Of course. Can you tell me what happened? I'll make a note of it and give it to the vet before he sees Sonny."

Sam ran through what had happened, giving the receptionist the same account she'd given her mother about the accident.

"Oh dear, poor thing. We'll get him up and running around in no time at all."

"I hope so. Thank you."

She ended the call and rang her mother.

"Hi, Sam. I'm in a meeting, is it important?"

"Sorry, Mum. Just to let you know Sonny has an appointment at two-fifteen. Thanks for doing this for me."

"I'll be there. Now don't you worry about him, he'll be fine once the vet has seen him."

"Love you, Mum. Will you let me know how he gets on?"

"Of course. I've got to go now, love."

Her mother hung up. Sam sat at her desk, still in a daze about what had gone on first thing. Bob rapped on the door and entered.

"Are you all right? You seem distant this morning."

She shrugged. "I'm fine. Sonny had an accident, and Mum is taking him to the vet's, so I'm going to be a little distracted today. I'm coming now." She left her desk and joined the rest of the team.

Bob handed her a cup of coffee, and she addressed the group. "Okay, let's up the ante today, folks. We've got a few things we need to chase up. The car involved in the hit-and-run has to remain our priority. Keep going over the discs, see what else we can glean from them. Try and get an enhanced image of the driver. His route to and from the scene. I don't want us to miss anything that might be in front of our eyes. This team goes above and beyond, let's maintain that perception others have of us."

"What about the why, boss?" Claire asked.

"The motive, yes. To both crimes. That's the major cause for concern I have. Why would someone kidnap Rory and not bother getting in touch with his wife to make some form of demand? And why would someone mow down her mother, intentionally killing her?" Sam said, adding a heavy sigh.

"Some kind of vendetta with the family?" Bob suggested.

Sam shrugged. "Such as what? If a request for money had presented itself then maybe I'd be inclined to think this was all about the kidnapping and maybe Lynne being targeted was down to the kidnapper getting his point across to the family. I've got huge doubts that's the bloody case in this instance, however, nothing else is coming to mind."

"Until we have the DNA results back, we're still shooting in the dark with our assumption that Rory was kidnapped, aren't we?" Bob asked.

"Yes, until a lot of the evidence points us in the right direction, that's all we have to hand for now. Which is why I stressed the importance of trawling through the footage again. Don't worry, I'll be chasing the lab hard today. The witnesses who called in about the Knoxs' day out, all intimated there was a tension between them, going back to my initial assumption that Fiona could be behind her husband's disappearance. While I still stand by that, the fact that her mother has now been murdered kind of puts the kibosh on that speculation. Nevertheless, I have nothing else to replace it with. Why? None of this makes any sense and is driving me nuts."

"The debt angle?" Claire suggested with a shrug.

"Possibly. A loan shark who needed to stress the importance on the family to pay up?" Sam said.

Bob vigorously shook his head. "Nope, not buying it. For a start, wouldn't it be Rory who is likely to take out the loan in the first place?"

"That's assumption on your part. I bet there are plenty of women out there who are desperate enough to go to a loan shark. Are you saying you believe the loan shark then went on to kill the mother?"

He flung his arms up in the air and then folded them tightly. "I don't know. I was just putting it out there."

Sam smiled at him. "I know. That's the frustrating part to this case, all this is pure speculation and none of it is adding up so far. I'm open to suggestions as to where we go from here, folks, if anyone is willing to share what's going on in their head." The room remained quiet. "See, that's just it, we're stuck in a rut. Therefore, the only answer is to keep digging, keep going over all the clues that have come our way so far and see if anything new comes to light."

"What about going back to see Fiona?" Bob asked.

"For what reason? I don't want to be seen to be hounding her. She's going through a tough time, her husband is missing and her mother has just been murdered. What state of mind do you think she's going to be in, dealing with all that shit, Bob?"

"Okay, but don't forget her husband is or was abusive. What if she got someone to deal with him?"

"We've checked her bank account, no large payments were on there."

"What if she got a friend to do it for her instead? What if she's having an affair and her lover has taken it upon himself to deal with Rory?" Bob suggested, crossing his arms.

"Those are pretty mighty ifs, partner. I'm not saying you're wrong, but she doesn't strike me as the type to cheat on her husband, no matter how he treats her. Maybe the way he treats her would be enough for her not to take that route in the first place, if you get what I mean? Anyway, that aside, that doesn't explain why Lynne is now sitting in a mortuary fridge, does it?"

He rolled his eyes. "I suppose. Sorry, just trying to think of solutions."

Sam smiled. "No need to be sorry. I'm not saying you're wrong. Maybe we'll go and see Fiona later on today, how's that?"

"Would it be worth checking her phone?" Bob asked.

Sam nodded. "Yes, okay, you get on and do that for me. Keep up with analysing the video footage, Alex."

He nodded. "Leave it with me, boss."

"I'll go and start hounding the lab for the results, we should have them by now."

"Give 'em hell," Bob called after her.

Sam considered his advice and rejected it by the time she sat in her seat. She rang the number and was passed through to the right department.

"Ah, Inspector Cobbs, I was in the process of looking up your phone number."

"I've saved you a job then, haven't I? Please tell me you have something for me?"

The tech guy laughed. "I have. It's as you suspected, the blood belongs to Rory Knox."

Sam sighed. "Okay, was there anything else showing up at the scene?"

"No, nothing. That's the only news I can share with you. I take it the man is still missing?"

"Yes. Answer me this, if you can: what are the chances of him still being alive, given the amount of blood he's lost?"

"It depends. The blood spread into the fabric, so he might not have lost as much as we first thought. Either way, he was bleeding when he left the scene, the wound would have needed attention. Whether he received what was needed is another question entirely."

"I get that. Thanks for rushing the results through for me." She left her desk and returned to her team to fill them in. "It was definitely Rory's blood. Although the tech guy said maybe there wasn't as much blood as we first thought, as it seeped into the fabric of the seat."

"Sounds logical to me. So he was bleeding when he left the car, with an average wound that would have needed to be attended to? Want me to check with the hospitals and doctors in the area?" Bob asked.

"Share the task around, Bob, there are too many for you to tackle on your own. Maybe the kidnapper took him to the doc's or hospital under a false name, don't get bogged down with looking for a Rory Knox. Would he have been seen by a doctor with no medical records? Just one more obstacle in our way."

Bob rolled his eyes. "Yeah, that thought never occurred to me, about using another name, I mean."

The phone on Claire's desk rang. She answered it and then raised her hand to gain Sam's attention.

She crossed the room to see what was going on. "What's up?"

"The car from the hit-and-run has been found."

Sam glanced sideways to see her partner earwigging the conversation. She turned her attention back to Claire. "Go on, surprise me, where is it? And what condition is it in?"

Claire's gaze drifted between Sam and Bob. "At the Morrisons' car park and yes, it's been burnt out."

Bob clicked his fingers. "I bet they've got CCTV footage of the incident."

"Claire, can you do the honours and ring the store to find out?"

"On it now, boss." Claire rang the supermarket and called out to Sam again once she'd hung up. "Yes, it happened at around midnight last night. There was a security guard on duty, he got a look at the driver who punched him in the stomach and legged it."

"Have you got the security guard's details?"

The ever-efficient Claire handed Sam a sheet of paper with a name and address on.

Sam winked at her. "Amazing, as always. Bob, grab your coat."

"What about all the chasing up I've got to do?"

Sam pointed at Claire's outstretched hand. "There's your answer. Let's get going."

8

They pulled up outside a block of council flats on the north side of Workington. "Number fourteen, where are you?" Sam jutted her head forward to get a closer look.

"Over there, at the end."

They left the car, and Bob knocked on the door to the flat.

The door opened to reveal a tall, thin man with stubble. "Yeah, what do you want?"

"Gary Brown?"

"That's right. If you're after your money, I get paid at the end of the week. I've told you before, I always pay you first before my rent. You need to stop hassling me."

Sam smiled at him. "Sorry, I should have introduced myself. I'm DI Cobbs, and this is my partner, DS Jones. All right if we come in and have a quick chat with you about the incident that happened at work last night?"

"Yeah, okay. You'll have to excuse the mess, the wife is away caring for the mother-in-law, she had a fall and broke her hip last week. I'm not used to looking after myself, so the place is a dive."

"Don't worry about it."

He showed them into a small lounge at the back which was dominated by a huge television. "Take a seat. Shove the papers and clothes on the floor. No, wait, I'll do it for you."

"Don't worry. We won't take up too much of your time. Can you tell us what happened?"

"Of course." He took a swig from a can of lager and placed it back on the floor beside him. "I was watching the delivery guys come and go on the security cameras when I saw this car draw up and park at the end of the car park. I zoomed in and saw the driver get out and take something from the boot and start pouring it over the car. I knew what the fucker was doing right away. I left my post, ran the length of the car park and grabbed hold of him before he could put a match to the vehicle. That's when the bastard took a couple of swipes at me. He rammed me in the gut with his head, doubled over I was, winded for a few minutes. Then he ran off, not before he set fire to the car, though. He bloody torched it, not caring if I was conscious or not and able to get away if the car exploded."

"Did you see in which direction he took off?"

"Yes, towards the main road, but that's all I can tell you. I was too concerned about my own safety to worry about what he was up to. I just made it back to the store, when boom! The car went up in smoke. Fancy someone torching a decent car like that, shame on them!"

"I agree. What about the assailant? Did you get a good look at him?"

"No. Sorry, he was wearing one of those macs with the hoods on, it was pulled tight around his head, and the car park down at that end was in darkness really, so I couldn't make out any significant features."

"I see. So he ran out of the car park towards the main road; did you see him get into another vehicle?"

"Nope. I was too intent on saving my own skin by then. I feel like I'm letting you down. Fuckers, oops, sorry, but people like that deserve to be hung, drawn and quartered. Why destroy it when there are needy people in the world?"

"Yes, it's terrible the lengths people covering up a major crime will go to."

Gary's eyebrows shot up. "Wow, I had no idea. What did the guy do?"

"We believe he was involved in a hit-and-run incident in town."

"Christ, I heard about that on the news. Didn't they say the woman had died from her injuries a few hours later?"

"That's the one. Horrendous crime. Okay, if there's nothing else you can tell us, we'd better be on our way."

"Did you pick up the footage from the store? Your forensic guys might be able to get something from it that I missed."

"We'll drop over and see the manager now. Thanks for the heads-up."

"Not a problem. I'll ring Max, the security guard on duty during the day, tell him to get the disc ready for you, if it'll help?"

Sam smiled and nodded. "Anything to save time, much appreciated, Gary. Are you back at work later?"

"Yep, I would never let a minor incident like this keep me off work. Need the money too much."

"You're to be admired. I fear some people in your situation would likely milk it to get extra time off. Stay there, we'll show ourselves out."

"Okay. Glad I could be of help with your investigation. Good luck trying to find the fucker."

"Thanks."

Sam and Bob left the flat.

"Why dump the car there?" Bob asked on the way back to the car.

"No idea. I'm wondering if he had another vehicle waiting for him for his getaway."

"Either parked up in the car park or someone else is involved and gave the bloke a lift."

Sam sighed and slipped behind the steering wheel. "Yet another piece of the puzzle intent on exasperating us. As we're this close to Fiona's, I think I'll pop around to see how she's doing."

"Might be good to drop in unannounced."

"You read my mind, partner. Buckle up." Sam started the engine and drew away from the flats. "Damn, hang on, we should go and pick up the footage from the supermarket first."

That's exactly what they did. As Gary predicted, Max, the daytime security guard, had the disc ready and waiting for them when they arrived. In the end, Sam had to double back and take a different route to get to Fiona's house.

Fiona opened the door with Summer in her arms. She gasped and added, "Oh God, have you found him?"

Sam raised her hand. "Sorry, no, we don't have any news yet. We were in the area and thought we'd drop by to see how you're doing."

"Come in. I wasn't expecting any visitors, and Summer's been having a whale of a time playing with all her toys in the front room. Do you want to come through to the kitchen instead?"

"Anywhere is fine by us."

They followed her through to the kitchen. Sam briefly glanced in the lounge on the way, and the mess was mind-blowing. "Ouch, that's going to keep you busy later, tidying that lot up."

"Yeah, much later. I'm not in the mood to deal with it now. The joys of having kids and constantly clearing up after them. I can't wait until she goes to playschool and someone else has to deal with the carnage she leaves in her trail." They all laughed. "Can I get you both a drink?"

"A coffee would be wonderful, thanks, Fiona," Sam said, pulling out a chair and sitting opposite so she could watch Fiona assemble the mugs and make the drink.

"Same for me. Two sugars, thank you." Bob sat next to Sam.

Fiona boiled the kettle, leaned against the worktop with her arms folded and asked, "Have you heard anything at all?"

"No, nothing whatsoever, which is infuriating as you can imagine. However, we did receive an interesting call this morning, telling us that the car involved in the hit-and-run had been found. We've just come from seeing a security guard at a supermarket who attempted to stop the driver. He got injured and couldn't really give us much. The car was torched, so I'm afraid whoever the culprit is, they did their best to cover up their DNA."

Fiona sighed heavily. "I was hoping you would have better news for me by now. Dare I ask how the tests are going on our car?"

"Ah yes, the DNA results came back this morning. They've managed to confirm the blood found on the front seat was that of your husband."

The colour drained from Fiona's cheeks. "Wasn't there a lot of blood found?"

"Yes, but please don't be alarmed by that. The forensic technician seemed to believe that it wasn't as bad as it first looked."

"Oh, why?" The kettle switched off, and Fiona poured the boiling water in the mugs, stirred them and distributed them. Fiona took her seat opposite and tilted her head. "Go on, I'm intrigued to know your theory."

"The tech guy reckons that the fabric in the seat will have soaked up the blood, making it look far worse than it actually was."

"So he didn't lose too much blood then, is that what you're saying?"

"Yes. At least that's the theory we're going on at the moment."

Fiona frowned. "Is that supposed to make me feel better?"

"We're taking it as a positive, I think you should, too."

Fiona cradled her mug in her hands and shook her head. "I don't think I can, I'm sorry, not after what happened to Mum. You say you've found the car, but what about the driver? Has he got away again?"

"For now. We've got his image on several cameras, it's only a matter of time before we catch up with him."

"How many more people have to either die or suffer in the meantime? Instead of being here with me, you should be out there, searching this town from top to bottom."

"We're doing our best, I promise you. Something that I've been meaning to ask you, is if you can think of anyone who might likely have a vendetta against your family. Not just you and your husband. I'm only asking this because of what happened to your mother. It's obvious we're dealing with the same perpetrator. It would be remiss of us not to consider the possibility."

Fiona shook her head. "I can't think of anyone, not someone who would deliberately abduct my husband and then kill my innocent mother. I'm at a loss to know who would do such a dreadful thing. We're simple people leading a simple life, or trying to."

"Okay, here's what is raising our suspicions. The fact that your husband asked around members of your family and his to lend him ten thousand pounds. I take it you're aware of that?"

"Yes."

"Did he get the funds, eventually?"

"Some, not all of it. Don't ask me from where, he refused to tell me."

"What about a loan shark, is that a possibility?"

Fiona stared at her mug and shrugged. "I suppose so. He didn't confide in me, ever. Kept most things to do with the running of the house to himself. I had no extra money myself. He put around eighty pounds in my bank account every week to buy the food. I wasn't allowed to spend more than that and had to take a calculator around the store with me, totting things up before I got to the checkout."

"I'm sorry he treated you like that, Fiona. Hard question to ask and an even harder one for you to answer, I suspect, but why did you stay with him? Suffer the abuse and not walk away?"

Fiona glanced up, tears misting her eyes. "How could I leave? He controlled everything I did. Restricted the visits I made to my family. Gave me just enough money for us to live on every week. Do you have any idea how much baby products cost? Like nappies, steriliser, wet wipes et cetera? It soon mounts up, especially when you have to buy the products regularly."

"I can imagine. Couldn't you have gone to a refuge centre for abused women?" Sam asked. She realised how hard it must be for some women to leave, but having a child must alter things significantly, at least it would in her mind.

"I couldn't bring myself to go to a place like that. He didn't beat me every day, not while I was pregnant anyway."

"What about since Summer's arrival?"

"Not regularly, sometimes yes, but nothing like it was before. It has been more verbal abuse lately, not physical."

"And that was okay with you? I don't mean that to sound condescending, I'm just trying to figure out why you didn't reach out to your family and friends more."

"I couldn't burden them with my problems. I'm not the type to do that. I had made my bed and needed to lie in it."

"I understand. But what a terrible existence you must have led on a daily basis."

Fiona ran a finger around the top of her mug. "I did. But I know there are women out there who are far worse off than I am. Repeatedly being put in hospital after taking a battering. It never got that bad."

Sam smiled at her. "It's not a competition as to who suffers more. Any time a man lays a hand on you, he's breaking the law nowadays. The police frown upon assault within a marriage and rate it up there with any other vile crime against a woman. We're doing our best to stamp out all forms of abuse in our communities. But we can't do it unless people like you come forward."

Fiona let out an ironic laugh. "You make it sound so easy."

"I know and I'm sorry if I'm coming across as a know-it-all but I'm speaking from the heart. No woman should be unhappy in her own home. Marriage is a partnership, the more women who realise that the better."

"I appreciate what you're saying, but it's so hard, you know, once you go down the abuse road, to have the courage to speak out against your husband. To make him stop. Maybe it's the mothers' fault?"

Sam frowned and inclined her head. "I'm not with you."

Fiona sighed. "It's just something that has occurred to me lately, that's all."

"What is?" Sam got the impression Fiona was about to clam up and keep her inner thoughts hidden.

"Every abusive man has a mother, right? If those women brought up their sons to love women and not disrespect them, then we wouldn't be in this situation, would we?"

Sam contemplated her words and even thought back to when she had interviewed Rory's parents. Cassandra had come across as a nice lady. "Maybe you have a point. Have you ever had any problems with Rory's mother in the past?"

"No, not really. Before her dementia set in, she tried to smother him with love and praise."

Fiona's mobile rang, she must have charged it since mentioning she rarely used it, and she jumped. She grabbed it from the worktop and looked at the caller ID. She turned the phone to Sam, her hand shaking. "Withheld number. What should I do? What if it's the kidnapper, the person who killed my mother? How will I cope? I can't speak to them, please don't make me."

"Do you want me to answer it?"

Fiona nodded and shoved the phone into Sam's outstretched palm. She motioned for Fiona to sit by her and held the phone between them so they could both hear what was being said.

Sam answered the phone. "Hello."

"Fiona, thank goodness you've answered, I was about to give up. This is Stan Burrows, Sophie's dad. I have some bad news for you."

"Oh no, what's wrong, Mr Burrows?" Fiona squeezed her eyes tightly shut to prepare herself.

"It's Sophie, she's in hospital." He paused to take a breath. "She was attacked last night."

Fiona shrieked. "No! Not my Sophie. How? Where?"

"As she left the pub, after work. She was on her way to the car when someone struck her from behind. Roger, the landlord, he's got it all on CCTV. He saw the attack and ran out to help her, but it was too late. The man ran off before he could get his hands on him. Roger called the police, they showed up, but they're worse than useless, told Roger they would search the area, but found nothing. I'm beside myself. I've not been well lately, with prostate cancer, I can barely move around the house, let alone get to the hospital. I wondered if you would go in my place. When she wakes up, she'll want to see a familiar face beside her."

"Of course, I'll go. I'm so very sorry that you're having to deal with this when you're so poorly. Is she in Whitehaven?"

"Yes, for now. They're assessing her there, but there's a chance she might get transferred to Carlisle later. I hope not, having her closer to me is more of a comfort than having her shifted miles away, out of reach completely. Oh God, what if she dies? I can't lose her, I just can't." Stan broke down and cried.

Fiona cried with him. "Please, don't think like that, Mr Burrows, we need to remain positive and strong. She's a fighter, she'll get through this with our love and help. I'll get to the hospital right away. Can I have your number? It's coming up as withheld. I'll contact you if there's any news."

"You're an angel, not sure what I would have done if you hadn't said yes." He read out his number, and Sam jotted it down in her notebook which she had withdrawn from her pocket.

Fiona reassured Stan that Sophie would be fine and hung up. She shook her head as more tears fell. "I can't handle any more of this. Not Sophie, why her? She's never harmed anyone in her life. If I lose her… well, she's like a sister to me. We went through school together, I've known her since I was five."

"I'm so sorry. Look, we can take you to the hospital, if you like?"

Fiona stared at Sam and nodded, then gasped. "I can't drag Summer down to the hospital again, it wouldn't be fair on her."

"Can you call a member of your family? Your father, sister perhaps?"

"No, I couldn't do that, they're dealing with enough shit at the moment. I wonder if Christine next door could watch her for a couple of hours."

"Why don't you ring her, or better still, pop around there and ask her in person? It might come across better if you did."

Fiona nodded and ran out of the back door. She returned within a few minutes. "Yes, she'll do it. I'll just gather a few things for Summer."

"Do you need a hand?" Sam offered.

"No, I'll be fine. Sorry to keep you waiting. I'll be as quick as I can."

"Don't worry, I'll make a few phone calls while you get your things together."

Fiona left the room and ran upstairs.

"You thinking there's a connection here?" Bob asked, his voice a low mumble.

"Don't you? That poor woman, she's beside herself. I'm going to ring the station, have a word with the person in charge of the case. Make them aware that there might be a connection."

Bob rolled his eyes. "Good idea. What's another case to handle on top of what we already have, anyway?"

"Stop whining. This is important, Bob. I need you to ring the team. Get Alex to go to the pub where Sophie works and ask him to pick up the disc so we can view the attack."

"Which pub was it?"

"Damn, hold fire until I speak to the copper in charge of the case." Sam rang the desk sergeant to make the relevant enquiries. She was then passed over to DS Brian King. She explained the situation to him. At first, he appeared reluctant to hand the case over. It wasn't until Sam insisted and threatened to go to his senior officer that he backed down. He told her the incident happened in the Queen Victoria's car park at just after eleven-thirty the night before. Sam thanked him and persuaded him to drop his notes off to her team in the incident room.

Fiona came back into the room ten minutes later, laden down with a bag stuffed with everything baby Summer was likely to need for the next few hours. "I won't be long now, so sorry to hold you up."

"You're not. Please, take your time." Fiona collected Summer from her playpen and went next door to her neighbour. She returned a few minutes later.

By this time, Bob had arranged for Alex and Liam to interview the landlord of the Queen Victoria and to pick up the footage for them to study when they eventually got back to the station, something which Sam was eager to do as she sensed the perpetrator was within reach now. But first, they had to drop Fiona off at the hospital to visit Sophie.

9

Another trip back to the Accident and Emergency Department, and Sam was more conscious about parking in an appropriate spot this time. The three of them entered the hospital, and the receptionist searched the database for Sophie's details.

"Ah yes, here she is. She's been taken to ICU. I'll contact the ward, let them know you're on your way up."

"Thanks. Which way is it?"

"To the end of the corridor, take the lift up to Level Three. Then follow the signs when you get out."

"We will." Sam smiled at the woman, and they set off.

Fiona hadn't spoken a word during the journey and was still lost in her own thoughts now.

"How are you holding up?" Sam asked once they'd hopped into the lift.

"I'm sorry to be so quiet. I'm struggling to get my head around all of this. My whole world has disintegrated within less than a week. How is one supposed to cope when that happens?"

"Hang in there. We're doing our very best to make sense of it all, I promise you."

Fiona's shoulders dipped. "It's so hard to fathom out what's going on. Is this about me? Does someone have it in for me?"

"Can you think of anything you've done over the years which might have upset someone enough to come after you and your family and friends in this way?"

"No. I've never hurt anyone, not intentionally anyway. This is all beyond me. I wish I had the answers; the truth is, I don't. God, I hope Sophie comes through this. We don't know how bad she is yet."

"You have to keep your thoughts positive. Hopefully, her boss coming out of the pub when he did saved her life. Speculation on my part, of course."

"If she dies… on top of losing Mum, and Rory going missing… I just don't know how I'm going to cope. My support network is dwindling faster than a greyhound running its first race."

"I know it probably feels like that. Let's not dwell on the negatives."

"Hard not to, given the evidence," Fiona replied. She stared up at the numbers of the floors as they lit up.

The doors pinged open, and they walked out of the lift.

Sam pointed to the right after reading the signs and noting that ICU was in that direction. Fiona's pace quickened the closer they got to the ward. They took the necessary precautions at the door. Put on robes and used the antibacterial gel before they entered the ward. A nurse smiled and came towards them. She held out her arm, preventing them from going any further.

"Can I help?"

Sam offered the woman her ID. "DI Sam Cobbs and my partner, DS Jones, and this is Fiona Knox. We're here to see how Sophie Burrows is."

"Okay, I'll allow the visit this time. We usually only permit two visitors at a time. I'm willing to make an exception when the police are involved. She's unconscious at present. Hasn't come around since she was brought in. The doctor has assessed her. She has a fractured skull and jaw, plus a couple of broken ribs. But looking on the positive side, she's still with us. I just wanted to warn you what to expect."

Fiona sobbed, and Sam placed an arm around her shoulders. "You don't have to do this, Fiona."

"I know. But I need to be here, I promised her father."

The nurse frowned.

"Her father has cancer. He hasn't got the strength to be with his daughter so he asked Fiona if she would come instead. They're like sisters, they've known each other for years."

"I see. Okay, let me take you to her. First of all, would you mind putting your phones on silent for me? It's not obligatory, but we do our best to give everyone peace and quiet while they're on the ward."

The three of them adjusted their mobiles, and then the nurse led them through the ward to the bed at the end, closest to the window, which had a curtain drawn around it. There was another nurse inside, noting down Sophie's vital signs.

"Nearly done in here. Won't be a second."

"Take your time, Sue," the nurse showing them the way replied.

Eventually, the nurse replaced the clipboard at the end of Sophie's bed and pulled back the screen to reveal a sorry sight. Fiona's legs gave way, and Sam was the first to react to save her from hitting the floor.

"Help me get her to the chair, Bob."

Her partner gripped Fiona's other arm, and under the gaze of the two surprised nurses, they led Fiona to the chair.

"Gosh, are you all right?" one of the nurses asked. "Can I get you a cup of tea?"

"Yes, please. It's the shock of seeing her like this. I'll be all right in a second or two."

"I'll be right back." Both nurses returned to their reception desk.

"She looks terrible. Who could do such a thing to my beautiful friend?" Fiona sobbed and reached for her best friend's hand.

The nurse returned a few seconds later and placed the cup and saucer on the bedside cabinet beside Fiona. "Two sugars, it's supposed to be good for shock. Give us a shout if you need us. I will add, she looks bad, but her vital signs are improving. I hope that's a source of comfort to you."

Fiona smiled and nodded at the nurse. "That's good to know. How long will it be before she wakes up?"

"Being unconscious is the body's way of helping her to heal. We'll keep a close eye on her, and hopefully she'll regain consciousness soon."

"I'll pray that's the case. She appears so badly broken. I can't bear to look at her in this state," Fiona replied, fresh tears emerging.

"Stay strong, if only for her sake. Sometimes talking to the patient can help the healing process along," the nurse advised.

"What shall I say to her?"

The nurse smiled. "Whatever is on your mind. Share past memories. Talk about her happy place. Her family, mention them if they're not able to visit. Anything along those lines. I'll leave you to it. Give either one of us a shout if you need us."

"Thank you," Fiona and Sam said in unison.

Fiona returned her attention to her friend. "Sophie, come back to us. I miss you. I'm sorry I haven't been in touch lately, but things have been getting on top of me for months, and I didn't want to burden you with my problems."

Sam listened and noted with interest what Fiona was saying but said nothing.

"Your dad sends his love. You've got to pull through this, he needs you more than ever, he told me that over the phone. Sophie, come on, you're a fighter. Don't let the person who did this get away with it. Come back to us, don't let him win. I need you in my life, now that my other confidante, my mother, has gone. Did you know she was dead? It was awful. But that's by the by, you're going to come through this, you have to. I'm ordering you to make it." She smiled and turned to face Sam. "I'm the bossy boots in our relationship, in case you're wondering."

Sam returned her smile. "I'm the same with my friends." She made a mental note to ring those she was close to. They hadn't been out in months, due to the renovations on the house, and she had lots of news to share with them, too.

The three of them stayed at the hospital for a couple of hours.

Fiona was hoarse from talking too much, she was doing so well in her attempt to bring her best friend back to them. Finally, Sam noticed one of Sophie's fingers move on the bed. She pointed it out to Fiona and then ran to get one of the nurses, who followed Sam back to check for herself.

"Yes, she's coming around. Sophie, are you with us?" the nurse asked in a singsong gentle tone.

Sophie groaned and finally opened her eyes. She closed them against the glare of the lights on the ward. "Where am I?" she whispered.

Fiona patted her friend's hand. "You're in hospital, love."

Sophie's head lolled to the side to face Fiona. "Where's my dad? I want my dad."

"He rang me, told me he didn't have the strength to come to the hospital, sweetie. He sends his love. I can ring him if you like?"

"Yes, please. I want to speak to him." Her free hand reached up and touched the bandages wrapped around her head. "It hurts so much. What's wrong with me?"

The nurse took up the conversation. "You were attacked, you have a fractured skull and jaw, it's only slight, enough for it to hurt, though. You also have a few cracked ribs, so be careful when you move."

While the nurse was seeing to Sophie, Fiona stared at her phone and then glanced up at Sam. She leaned over and said, "My father rang twenty minutes ago. I should call him back."

"I agree. I'll dial Sophie's father on my phone."

Fiona nodded and left her seat. Sam removed her notebook from her pocket and rang Sophie's father. He answered on the first ring.

"Hello, Mr Burrows, I'm DI Cobbs. I'm here at the hospital with your daughter. Hold the line, please."

Sam smiled and handed her phone to Sophie. "Daddy, I'm okay. Please don't worry about me. I'm in safe hands. I'll be home soon… no, don't you dare get upset. I need you to take care of yourself. I'm all right."

Sam was half-listening to Sophie's conversation when Bob nudged her knee and gestured for her to look at Fiona who had gone deathly white. Sam leapt out of her chair and demanded to know what had happened.

"It's my sister, Donna. She's gone missing. Dad has tried and tried to contact her, and there's no answer from her phone. He found her car unlocked and the keys still inside, but she's nowhere to be seen. Oh God, this can't be happening. Not more bad news."

Sam held out her hand and spoke to Fiona's father. "Mr Chanters, it's DI Cobbs. Where are you?"

"Donna and I had arranged to meet outside Donaldson's Undertakers to discuss the funeral arrangements for my wife, but she's gone. Please, you have to help me. I can't find her. I need my daughter back."

"Okay. I'm going to need you to remain calm." Sam clicked her fingers to gain Bob's attention. "Bob, get onto the station. I want several patrol cars sent to Donaldson's Funeral Home ASAP, tell them we'll meet them there." She returned to her call. "Sorry, Mr Chanters, help is on the way. We'll get to you soon. Hang tight."

"I'll do my best. Please, you have to find her. I don't want to be making arrangements for two funerals. This week has been hard enough on us all as it is. You have to help me find my daughter."

"Don't worry. It's all in hand. Give us ten minutes to get to you."

10

Sophie insisted that Fiona should leave and be with her father who needed her more. En route, Fiona rang Sophie's father to explain what had happened and that, at Sophie's insistence, she was having to put her own family first. Mr Burrows, although disappointed, said that he completely understood and thanked her for visiting his daughter. Fiona assured him that she would return to the hospital as soon as her sister had been found. If she was ever found!

Sam instructed Bob to drive while she made several calls to the station. Her heart rate matched her racing mind, accompanied with dark, disturbing thoughts. *Has the kidnapper struck again? It seems likely if Donna's car was found with the keys still in the ignition. If she hasn't been abducted then why would she leave the vehicle and neglect to meet her father, even though her car was found in the vicinity?*

Again, Sam had far more questions than answers running through her head at this worrying time. What the hell was going on? As far as Fiona was concerned, there was no logical reason as to why someone would go about trying to destroy her family. Without any form of motive to go on, they were in chaos. There *had* to be a reason. But what? And why hadn't there been a ransom demand for Rory by now? Were they going to stumble across his body in the near future? Her suspicions turned to Fiona once more; maybe the kidnapper had her by the short and curlies, was threatening that if she spoke to the police, they would kill Rory. She had to admit, sometimes she struggled to make out what Fiona was either thinking or feeling.

Sam glanced in the rear-view mirror at Fiona as they travelled. Yes, there were tears and she seemed fraught, but were they real? Maybe Fiona was a good actress, able to pretend that she was upset at the drop of a hat.

Fiona caught Sam looking at her and offered up a weak smile.

"We'll be there soon," Sam felt the need to say.

"I'm so worried about Donna. What if the person who kidnapped Rory has got her as well? What if he's taken them both and killed them somewhere? What if...?"

"Fiona stop! There are too many what-ifs you can summon up. Let's try and deal with the facts, rather than mere speculation that might tear you apart. Have faith in us. If there are any clues to discover, we'll find them and go from there, okay?"

"Yes. I'm sorry. It's so difficult for my mind not to imagine all sorts. Especially after what has happened so far. Mum dying, Sophie almost dying, and now my husband and my sister both missing. For all we know, at the mercy of a madman. Why? That's what I'm struggling to get my head around."

"There has to be a reason why your family has been targeted in this manner. I know I keep asking you if you can think of anyone with a vendetta against either you or your family, but honestly, that's the only thing I can think of right now. As far as we know, the person involved in all three crimes against your family and friends has left no evidence for us to follow up on. All we have is Rory's blood at the scene where your car was dumped. I'll chase up the lab later, see if they've stumbled across a hair or anything else to help us, but the last time I spoke to a lab technician, he told me they hadn't discovered anything else out of the ordinary."

Fiona shook her head. "I just don't know what to say. I've thought and thought, but nothing is coming to mind. I'm not the type to fall out with people or anger anyone just for the sake of it."

They rounded the corner and saw the road cordoned off and a diversion sign blocking it. "Pull up here, Bob. We'll walk the rest of the way."

After parking in an available space, the three of them strode over to where two patrol cars were parked.

"Dad. I'm here. Are you all right?" Fiona shouted, her voice breaking on a sob.

Father and daughter hugged. Mr Chanters seemed old and weary. "I'm okay, sweetheart. I can't believe she's gone missing."

"I know. It's terrible, Dad. In the car on the way over here, we were trying to think of a reason why the family is being targeted like this, but came up blank. I don't suppose you have any ideas, do you?"

His gaze dropped to the ground, and he shook his head. "No, I really can't think of anything. Your mother and I have led a pretty uneventful life over the years. Do you think this is anything to do with Donna? She's had a few troubled souls for boyfriends in the past, hasn't she?"

Sam's ears pricked up at the suggestion.

"I suppose so, but they were years ago. Nothing recent, Dad."

"It doesn't matter," Sam interrupted the father-daughter conversation. "If there's something that's troubling you, Mr Chanters, we need to know what that is. It could prove to be the link we've been searching for."

He stared at Fiona for a couple of moments and then looked at Sam. "Donna got involved with a couple of men who were partial to taking drugs. This was back in her teens. You know how young girls are, they always appear to be drawn to the bad boys in our society. I told her she had to make a choice, them or us. Happened twice, it did. You would have thought she'd have learnt the first time, but no, young girls always think they know best. She didn't."

"I'm going to need to sit down with you, go through what happened in detail, if you don't mind?"

"If I must. Is that what you believe has happened? One of these bastards has crawled out of the woodwork and is now taking his revenge on the family?"

"It's something that we need to delve into further, given that we're struggling to find anything else to focus on."

"Very well. Fiona, you're going to need to help me. I struggle to remember names as it is at my time of life."

Fiona nodded. "Okay, why don't we start with Dennis... what was his surname now?"

Bob extracted his notebook and waited with his pen poised.

"Dennis Shaw or Sharp, was it? Can I come back to that one in a moment?"

Sam smiled. "Yes, no pressure. Was there someone else you can think of?"

"Yes, there was that one who had spiked hair, like a punk rocker, Fiona, you remember him. I seemed to recall he gave you the creeps, didn't he?" Mr Chanters said. He ran a shaky hand through his short grey hair.

"That was Neil, I think. Neil Bradley," Fiona replied.

Sam nodded and smiled. "Excellent, that's going to help us a lot. I don't suppose you can remember where both of them lived?"

Without hesitation, Fiona told them, "One in the Whitehaven area and the other in Workington, I believe. But we're going back at least six years or more, so the possibility of them having moved on is fairly high, I should imagine."

"It's okay, it gives us a good foundation to go on. Dennis Shaw or Sharp? Can you try and narrow it down for me?"

Fiona paused. "Thinking about it, it was Shaw, definitely. His mother used to own a hairdressing salon in the Whitehaven area, if that helps?"

"It could do. I'll get my team on it now, see what they can come up with. Excuse me a moment." Sam stepped away from the father and daughter to place the call. "Claire, it's me. I need you to try and find two possible suspects for me. A Dennis Shaw from Whitehaven, his mother owned a hairdresser's in the area a few years ago, which might help, and a Neil Bradley from Workington. Sorry, that's all I have on him. Both men used to go out with Fiona's sister, Donna. They're the only ones the family can come up with who might have any grievances with them."

"Leave it with me, boss. I'll give you a tinkle back."

"Thanks, if you can prioritise the request for me, even better."

"I'll get cracking on it now."

"Great. Thanks, Claire."

Sam headed back towards Bob, Fiona and her father but veered off to speak with a uniformed officer who was talking to a couple of members of the public. She showed her warrant card and introduced herself. "Hello, there. I'm SIO on a case concerning the family. What do we have?"

The officer smiled at the couple he was talking to and took a few steps to his right. Sam followed.

"The couple run one of the shops on the other side of the road. They saw the young woman pull up in her car. Soon after, a man wearing a balaclava approached the vehicle. He yanked the door open and forced her to go with him."

Sam shook her head, gobsmacked. "Wow, in broad daylight?"

"Yes, that's what I found hard to believe, too, ma'am."

"I'm going to have a word with them, is that okay?"

The officer nodded. "Feel free."

They walked back to the couple. "Thanks so much for ringing the police. Would you mind going over the details again, with me?"

The couple in their sixties were holding hands. The woman clung to her husband's arm with her other hand as well. "It was so shocking for us to witness." She told Sam what the officer had already relayed and added, "My husband shouted at the man to stop and told him that he'd called the police."

"That was brave of you. What was the man's reaction?"

Her husband scoffed. "He gave me the finger and said, 'Up yours, you old fart'. Bloody cheek. If I'd been fitter, I would have run after him. I've got a dicky heart, you see. It prevents me from overexerting myself. I feel guilty not being able to save that poor woman. Saying that, no one else bothered to help her, only us. We did the best we could."

"And we're grateful for your intervention, sir. Are you sure the abductor was a man?"

He scratched his head and glanced down at his wife. "What do you think, Sue?"

She nodded. "Oh, definitely. He was wearing snug jeans over narrow hips and a man's jacket. He was a lot taller than the woman, and there was just something about his build that screamed he was male and not to mention his voice when he spoke."

"That's good enough for me. Can you describe the colour of his jacket and jeans?"

"Let me think," the woman said. "Ah, yes, it was one of those combat jackets I think you call them, and his jeans were faded blue. They had a few holes in them, too, at the knees. Bloody trend, that is, I feel myself reaching for my sewing kit every time I see someone wearing a pair."

Sam smiled. "Yes, the fashion today leaves a lot to be desired, I agree. Did you see what happened to them after he dragged her out of the vehicle?"

Her husband jumped in and said, "The girl put up a bit of a fight. The bloke hit her and shouted in her face, told her to behave or he'd kill her. It subdued her enough for him to steer her away. They went that way. Turned right into Sandalwood Road and, from there, I haven't got a clue. I'm sorry. My attention was focussed on getting hold of the police. Left me and the wife shaking, it did. Horrendous ordeal, never witnessed such brutality in all our lives, have we, love?"

"No, never. Tell us you're going to do your best to find her. I dread to think what might happen to the woman if he hangs on to her."

"We're going to do our very best. You've been most helpful. Try not to worry about it too much. We'll action an alert, and all cars will be on the lookout for the man, I can assure you."

"Thank goodness," the woman said with a glimmer of a smile.

"Take care of each other."

"We will," the man replied. "We're going to shut up shop and spend some quality time together, we work far too hard. Let's face it, you never know what's around the corner, do you?"

"True enough. Try not to worry about things, though." Sam smiled to reassure the couple and returned to her partner's side. "She was abducted by a man, by what the couple said. I think the man likely followed her to the location and then made his move once Donna had parked up. He struck her to keep her compliant, and they headed off in that direction. He probably had a car waiting for him around the corner."

Bob frowned. "Are you saying he knew she was going to park up here?"

Sam considered his question for a moment. "Possibly. Either that or he was following her, saw her indicate and park up, then reversed around the corner and approached her on foot. That's the best I can come up with off the top of my head."

"Maybe you're right. Want me to do the rounds with the shops, see if any of them have got cameras installed?"

"Yes, that'd be great, Bob. Thanks."

Bob set off on his mission, and Sam moved closer to join Fiona and her father who were consoling each other. "Try not to get yourselves worked up. I know that's easy for me to say, but I'm going to circulate the information we have gathered from the witnesses I've just spoken to."

"They saw what happened?" Mr Chanters asked, a hopeful shine to his eyes.

"Yes. They tried to intervene the best they could, but the man has a heart problem and thought it best not to get too involved. They rang us as soon as they could, which is a blessing."

"I understand. Could they tell you much?"

"Only that Donna pulled up and a man yanked the door open and dragged her from the car. Then he marched her up the road and around the corner. I suspect he had a car waiting there."

"So he knew she was coming here to meet me? How is that possible?" Mr Chanters asked.

"That's something I can't tell you, sir, I'm sorry. Bob has gone in search of any possible footage available from the shops around here. We can use that to try to identify the perpetrator."

"How exactly?" Mr Chanters frowned.

"We can compare his profile to what we have already, that'll be a start, and it will tell us if we're dealing with the same person or may even throw another possibility into the mix, that there is more than one person involved."

"I understand. This is all too distressing for us, Inspector. It seems to be one thing after another at the moment. How are we supposed to cope with all of this?"

Sam sighed. "By hanging in there. Maybe you should consider sticking together, for now. Safety in numbers could possibly be the key."

"You mean in case this person comes after either of us?"

"Yes."

Mr Chanters flung an arm around his daughter's waist. "I think she's right, love. Shall we give it a go?"

Fiona nodded. "I agree. Do you want to stay at my house, Dad, it might be easier, what with Summer's stuff being there?"

"I was about to suggest the same." He smiled and kissed his daughter's cheek. "Oh no, I'm going to have to attend the appointment with the funeral home first. I'm late as it is."

"We're going to have to head back to the station anyway. SOCO are on their way. We'll wait for them to arrive before we leave. I'm sure the undertaker will be compassionate given the circumstances. Why don't you both go there now?"

"She's right, Dad. They're hardly going to reprimand us for turning up late, are they? After that we can go back to your house, collect an overnight bag and go back to my place. Summer is going to be in her element with you around to make a fuss over her."

"The one bright moment in all of this, I suspect. Come on then, let's get this daunting task over with and let the inspector get on with her job of trying to find your sister and your husband. Will you keep in touch with us, Inspector?"

"You have my word, sir. Stay safe. Any problems, ring me, you've got my number; that means day and night, okay?"

"We'll do that."

Sam watched Mr Chanters and Fiona walk towards the funeral home a few doors away. It stuck in Sam's throat that Donna was so close to being safe before she was abducted.

Bob nudged her elbow. "Are you all right?"

She blew out a breath and shook her head. "Not really. I feel guilty for not protecting the family more."

"How could you know this was going to happen?"

"Logic should have told me to have put something in place to keep them safe. Now it's too bloody late."

"If you feel like that, why don't you suggest Fiona and her dad move into a safe house?"

She turned and gave him a thoughtful nod as her mind tore up a storm. "You're right, I should do that. Let's get back to the station first, and I'll organise things from there." With that, the SOCO techs turned up just beyond the cordon which had been erected. "Let me have a word with them, tell them what I need, and we'll shoot off."

"I'm going to check what's around the corner, maybe there are more cameras around there to help us."

"Good idea."

Sam waited for the tech guys to sort out their equipment, and then she gave them a rundown of what they were dealing with and what she needed from them. By the time she'd finished, Bob was back and waiting by the car.

"Let me know what you find ASAP, if you would, gents."

"Don't worry, we will. It's going to be a few days, Inspector, so don't go holding your breath," one of the techs replied.

"Thanks. Do your best for me." She left them to it and walked towards the car. Once they were inside, she asked her partner, "Well, any good?"

"I knocked on a couple of doors, and a bloke saw the man putting Donna in the boot of his car."

"Okay. Did he try to stop him? Or is that me asking too much of the public to get involved?"

"He feels like he let her down, he can barely walk, boss. I actually spoke to him through the window of his lounge. He had one of those walking frames, so I wouldn't be quick to lay any blame at his door."

"Fair enough, I take it back. Tell me he was able to describe the car."

"Yep, a silver Ford."

Sam turned to face him and gestured at him with her hand to add more. Sadly, Bob shook his head. "Damn. We'll never bloody find them."

"It's not like you to be so negative."

Sam leaned forward and rested her head on the steering wheel. "This case is driving me nuts. Why is nothing slotting into place? We've usually got something significant we can latch on to by now, right now we've got nothing."

"Don't beat yourself up. We can only investigate any evidence or clues that come our way and, as it stands on this one, that's very little so far."

"Which means we're dealing with someone either very intelligent or super professional."

Bob sighed. "Yep. We won't know which until we bloody get hold of the bastard. If we get our hands on him."

"God, don't say that. We can't be negative, that's not going to help our cause, is it?"

"Hard not to be, given what has gone on this week," her partner countered.

Sam sat upright and started the engine.

One frigging break, that's all we need. Is it too much to ask?

11

He watched and waited for the area to become quiet. Around three that afternoon his wait was over. Getting out of the car, he went to the boot and removed his captive. He'd placed a bag over her head so she had no idea where she was going.

"Please, don't do this," she muttered.

Disguising his voice, he warned, "Scream and it'll be the last thing you do. I'll kill you then return to kill the rest of your family, you hear me?"

Donna nodded her compliance and sniffled. "I'm sorry. I'll do what you say. Please don't hurt me."

"Keep that gob shut and I won't. Keep talking and you're going to wish you hadn't. Got that?"

"Yes."

He steered her across the open ground to the entrance. The shaft was just as he remembered it, sinister in the darkness, even by the entrance. He opened the gate and prodded Donna in the back. "Get in."

"Where are we? What are you going to do to me?"

He yanked her arm, pulled her close to him and growled in her ear, "Something wrong with your bloody hearing?"

"No. I'll keep quiet."

The lift jerked into action and took them down into the depths of the old mineshaft. He'd had his eye on this place for some time, while he'd been formulating his scheme. His friend used to work here, had brought him here numerous times before it was closed down. He had no idea if he'd be able to gain access to the area or not, until last week. He'd chanced his arm and found it only partially boarded up; he'd removed some of the boards, and bingo! The place wasn't as bad as he'd imagined. An ideal spot to keep someone against their will. To dispose of a body or two, if needed.

Could this week get any better? He didn't think so. Everything so far had gone according to plan. He hoped the rest of his plans slotted into place just as well.

The lift juddered to a halt, and Donna toppled into him. He pushed her upright, couldn't stand the bitch that close to him. Opening the small gate, he wrenched on her arm to get her moving. "Mind your head. Keep low."

"What? Why?"

He walked forward. Donna immediately bashed her head into the rock face that was jutting out beside her. "Ouch. What the fuck was that?"

"What did I tell you? Perhaps you'll listen to my warnings next time."

"I will. It would be better if you removed the hood."

"Shut the fuck up. Just duck down and keep your trap shut. We're nearly there now."

He guided her through the narrow passage. On the way, she managed to bang her head a few more times before they reached the room where he intended to keep her. Far enough away from the lift so that if she escaped, which he doubted was a possibility, she wouldn't know which direction to go in to achieve safety.

He removed the hood once he'd shoved her into one of the chairs at the Formica table. This was where the workers used to come for a rest during their shifts. A reprieve from all the hard work they put in during their shift down this hellhole.

"Where are we? Who are you? What do you want from me?"

"Questions, questions, so many damn questions." He slammed his hand on the table, making her jump. "Can't you ever keep that big trap of yours shut?"

"Do I know you?"

She stared at him, trying to figure out if she could recognise him through the balaclava he was wearing.

He turned away, disliking the spotlight being on him. It made him uncomfortable. Disguising his voice still, he ordered. "Put your hands out."

She did as she was instructed and placed her hands down, intertwined on the table in front of her. He bound her wrists with rope.

She flinched a couple of times. "Ouch, that hurts."

"It's supposed to. You even consider escaping, and I'll slit your throat, you hear me?"

"Yes. I won't. What do you want from me? Are you the same person who has been persecuting my family this week? Who kidnapped my brother-in-law and killed my mother?" Her voice caught on a sob at the mention of her mother.

"That's me. And now I have you in my grasp. Oh, what fun we're going to have. Just you and me."

"What? Where's Rory, what have you done with him?"

"Ah, wouldn't you like to know?" He let out an evil laugh, muffled slightly by the woollen balaclava.

Donna shrank back, fear resonating in her eyes. He had her where he wanted her at last. Away from her family, unable to interfere with the ongoing investigation. *Will she be out of sight, out of mind?*

Next, he bent down and tied her ankles together then left her to her own devices.

"No, you can't leave me here, you just can't. What will I do for food? You haven't left me any water. I won't be able to survive without it. Please, don't do this. Tell me what you want and I'll do it."

"I want you to keep your ruddy mouth shut. No chance of you doing that, though, is there? I'll be back later with supplies. You and I can get properly acquainted then. I'm recording everything that goes on down here." He pointed at a round camera in the corner, he'd rigged up a few days earlier. "You try to shout out or even think about escaping, and I'll be back here like a shot, to kill you."

Donna gasped. "I won't. There's no need to go that far. Please, just tell me why you're doing this to me."

He smiled beneath the mask. "Because I can. Call it retribution, if you like."

"For what? Has my family wronged you in some way?"

He laughed, removed his hood and laughed again at the stunned look on her face. He then left the room, locking the door behind him.

12

It was all go for Sam and Bob when they arrived back at the station. The first task Sam tackled was trying to find a safe house for Fiona and her father. She failed dismally. She couldn't have chosen a worse time; apparently, there was a huge drugs case going on in the area, and all the houses they normally used for protecting witnesses were currently unavailable. "Shit! That's no good to us," she complained, the second Bob popped into the room with a cup of coffee for her.

"What other options are there? To put an officer outside Fiona's gaff?"

Sam clicked her fingers and pointed at him. "Yes, we'll do that. I'll have a word with Nick, see if he can organise it right away." She lifted the phone and rang the desk sergeant who was only too happy to oblige and assured her that within the hour, an officer would be stationed outside the house, around the clock.

Relieved, she hung up and said, "All sorted. One less thing to worry about. How have the team been getting on?"

"Claire managed to track down the mother of Dennis Shaw. She said her son passed away from a drug overdose two years ago, so I suppose we can scrub his name off the list."

"No! You reckon?" she replied, a sarcastic grin emerging. "What about Bradley? Any news on him?"

"Nope, she's still trying to locate him."

Sam sighed. "Okay. Have you had a chance to run through any of the footage found at the scene today?"

"I have. We've got the incident in all its glory. Want to take a butcher's?"

Sam left her chair, picked up her cup and followed her partner back into the incident room. "Show me."

Bob switched the large TV screen on and tapped on his keyboard. The scene materialised on the screen for all the team to view. "Hmm… she pulled up and almost immediately he was there, despite his car being parked around the corner."

"Therefore, we have to presume he knew where she was going. The question is, how?" Sam frowned and shook her head.

"Could he be listening to her phone calls?" Suzanna asked.

Sam nodded slowly. "Possibly. I'd say he definitely had her under surveillance."

"Maybe we're looking at the wrong person here," Bob suggested. "Maybe the father's phone has been tapped and not Donna's."

"Good point. Either way, the abductor knows the family. We just need to fathom out how, and let's be honest, that has sidestepped us so far."

"All right if I interrupt, ma'am?" Alex piped up.

Sam turned to face him. "Go on."

"We've already established that he followed her to the location; do you want me to check the ANPR and CCTV in the immediate area, see if I can pick up Donna's car?"

Sam nodded. "Yes, I'm with you. If we can manage to locate her car then we can see who was following her."

"Exactly. Just trying to think outside the box, boss."

"Good shout, Alex. Let me know what you find."

"I'll get on it now."

"What else do we have?" Sam asked the rest of the team.

"Nothing much, is the honest answer," Claire admitted with a sigh.

"I'm still searching for anything to do with Bradley. I've done my best. My guess is that he's no longer in the area."

"Always a possibility. Don't give up. Bob, can you call Rory's Aunt in Torquay? That's one lead we didn't chase up. See if he's shown up there at all. I'm going to ring the hospital, see if Sophie Burrows is fit enough to speak to me yet." Sam dipped back into her office and rang the ICU.

"ICU, how can I help?"

"Hi, this is DI Sam Cobbs, we probably met earlier. I came to see Sophie Burrows."

"Ah yes, I remember, you had to leave suddenly, on an emergency. What can I do for you, Inspector?"

"That's right. I was calling to see how Sophie was and whether she would be up to answering any questions about her attacker?"

"I think you're going to have to wait a few days before she's well enough to do that, I'm afraid. It hit her hard when you left. She's very tired due to suffering from what we call long Covid. The upshot is, her body needs to recover a little more before we can class her as being out of the danger zone."

"Ah, yes, I should have considered that. Forget I asked. I'll keep in touch, if that's okay?"

"Of course it is. Goodbye."

Disappointed, Sam replaced the phone in its docking station and contemplated what to do next. She reached for the phone again and called Jackie Penrose, the press officer. "Hi, Jackie, I need another favour, and quickly."

"Another press conference, I'm guessing," Jackie replied.

"Yes, we've got a second member of the same family who has been kidnapped. This time it's the sister of the woman whose husband has already gone missing."

"Oh, shit! That's not good at all. Let me see what I can do and get back to you soon."

"You're a star, thank you."

Sam ended the call and returned to the incident room. "Do you have anything else for me, guys? I've put the wheels in motion to make another appeal for the public's help on this one."

"I've analysed all the footage we have from the cameras on the route Donna took this morning and found her car. Following her was a silver Ford Puma." Alex tapped his keyboard and pointed at the TV screen on the wall. "As you can see, the image is a little grainy. I'm trying to improve the quality, but it might be a case of handing it over to the lab for them to do."

Sam tutted. "Do your best, Alex, time is of the essence, and you know how long we're likely going to have to wait for the lab to get back to us. Something is telling me we haven't got long, what with Donna being abducted as well as Rory."

"I'll keep trying to improve it. One thing I've noticed, though… bear with me while I bring everything up." He clicked on a few buttons, and the screen split in half and then quartered. "Here we're looking at all the footage we've managed to cobble together so far, of the perp or perps. Some images cleaner than others thrown into the mix. I've been comparing the images for around fifteen minutes now and, to me, they appear to be the same person."

Sam nodded and slapped a hand on Alex's shoulder. "Excellent news to get that confirmation, Alex. Now, about the Ford, can you tell when the car began following Donna?"

He smiled and raised a finger. "I managed to locate Donna's car right back to where she set off from work at the pharmaceutical company, and this is what I found." He pointed to the lower corner of the screen, at the Ford leaving a parking space opposite the gates to the entrance.

"Wow, he was clearly waiting for her. So what are we to take from this? That he knows her? Knows her routine? Has he had her under surveillance for a while?"

"By that I take it you want me to check the ANPRs from prior days?" Alex asked.

"I think it would be negligent of us not to, don't you agree?"

Alex nodded. "I'll get onto it now, boss."

Sam smiled and moved around the room to her partner. "What about the aunt in Torquay, any luck there, Bob?"

His expression clouded over. "Wish I hadn't bothered calling her, or, put it this way, had I visited her in person and she'd spoken to me the way she did, I would have wrung her scrawny neck," he replied, disgruntled.

Sam found it hard to suppress a giggle. "That's presuming she has a scrawny neck in the first place. What did she say?"

"That the reason she moved down to the south-west was to get away from her damn family."

"Did she mention why?"

"She owned several beauty salons in the area, not just one, and Rory in particular used to suck up to her for money. At first, she found his requests *charming*, her words not mine, but after a while, him getting out the begging bowl every couple of months wore her down. I tried to ask her several more questions, but she was having none of it. She didn't want to know. In the end, she hung up on me. Not before she shed some angry tears, though."

"I see. Things must have been bad if she felt the need to up sticks and leave her successful businesses behind."

"Yep, that thought crossed my mind, too. I tried to call her back, you know, to apologise for upsetting her, but she refused to answer." He shrugged.

"Never mind. If anything, it proves how selfish Rory is yet again. Wanting, or should I say expecting, his family to bail him out."

"Yeah, in the end he got so desperate he obtained the money elsewhere, rather than turn to a loan shark."

Sam chewed on her lip. "We still don't know that's the truth, as yet. Thinking about it logically, if he'd successfully got the loan then why was he still overdrawn at the bank? It doesn't add up."

"Maybe he had other debts floating around and paid off the ones he thought were more important."

"Perhaps. Anyway, it's something to consider going forward. I'm just waiting on Jackie to organise the press conference and get back to me."

"Sounds like a plan."

"In the meantime, I'm going to chase up Nick, make sure he's sent a uniformed officer over to Fiona's house. She and her father should be there by now. We left them over an hour ago."

"It takes time to organise a funeral. My guess is they won't be there yet."

"We'll see. I'll be back in a tick." Sam went through to the office to place the call. Nick assured her that an officer had been dispatched to Fiona's address but the family weren't at home. "They should be back soon. Tell him to wait in the car until they arrive."

"Already told him to do that, ma'am."

"Let me know if anything happens, when it happens, Nick."

"You'll be the first to know."

She relaxed in her chair, relieved that every angle of the case was now covered by her team, but then the reality struck that they were no further forward, not really. The phone on her desk rang, interrupting her thoughts.

"DI Cobbs, how…?"

"It's me. How does three o'clock sound to you?" Jackie said cheerfully.

"Sounds like you've worked your magic for me yet again. Thanks so much, Jackie. I'll see you then."

"You will indeed. It's always a pleasure."

Sam smiled and attacked her paperwork with vigour, knowing that her team were on the ball and had every base covered, to the best of their ability.

An hour later, Sam met Jackie downstairs in the press conference room as it filled up with journalists from the TV and the newspapers. She leaned in close to Jackie and said, "Good turnout. I can't thank you enough for organising this so quickly."

Jackie smiled and hitched up a shoulder. "It's all in a day's work for me."

"I've made a few notes. I hope they don't ask any awkward questions."

"Such as? Anything in particular you're trying to avoid?" Jackie asked, keeping her own voice low to avoid any of the journalists nearby picking up on what they were saying.

"I didn't tell you over the phone but, as well as the two kidnappings, the mother of the woman who was abducted this morning was recently killed in a hit-and-run."

"Shit! I had no idea. I remember seeing the incident on the news yesterday. Oh my, that poor family. Do you have any idea who is persecuting them like this?"

"Not a bloody clue. This man is doing his very best not to let us catch up with him, changing vehicles, destroying the cars he has no further use for."

Jackie shook her head. "And in the process, getting rid of any possible DNA evidence, is that it?"

"Yep, that's what we're up against. Pain in the rear at times. All we seem to be doing is chasing our tails on this one."

"What about the other members of the family? Are they being protected now?"

"Yes. The father and daughter are together at one house with a copper standing guard outside. I tried to get them into a safe house, but there's a massive drugs case going to court next week and all the valuable witnesses are tucked up in the only safe houses available to us."

"Ah yes. I know the case you're referring to. Vile bloody gang. Umm... that's not to say your case isn't as bad."

After Sam and Jackie held the conference, Sam made her way back upstairs to the incident room. The conference left her feeling drained and depressed. All the damn journalists appeared to be interested in was what Sam and her team were doing about finding out who had murdered Fiona's mother. Feeling backed into a corner, Sam had decided to call the conference to an abrupt halt. There were times when there could be too many journalists in one room. Seemingly getting braver with their antics in the crowd. Frequently turning a conference on its head and asking questions that the SIO found impossible to answer, instead of listening to the facts and doing their utmost to help find the culprits.

That was often the daunting task of dealing with the press. When they got their claws into something, they were worse than a lion stalking its prey in the wilderness.

"I need a coffee," Sam stated, barging into the incident room.

Bob leapt out of his seat to oblige.

"Any news while I've been gone?"

The team were all silent and looking at Bob for guidance.

"You're going to need this." He placed the coffee on the desk in front of her.

"Go on. Why am I getting a bad feeling about this? Don't tell me either Donna's or Rory's body has been found?"

Bob shook his head. "Nope. You're way off the mark."

"Come on, Bob. Get on with it, the suspense is churning up my insides. What's going on?" Her gaze drifted around the team, and some of them averted their eyes.

"I've only just put the phone down. I was gearing myself up to come and tell you the news."

Sam gesticulated for him to hurry up.

"Fiona's father called asking for help…"

Sam raised a hand. "Where was he calling from?"

Bob raised an eyebrow. "You're going to have to let me finish, boss. As I said, he rang us, from Fiona's house. In a right state, he was. Someone managed to get into the house, knocked him unconscious and took Fiona and the baby."

"Fuck! You're kidding me. How is that possible when there's an officer guarding the house?"

"Fiona's father found the officer lying on the front doorstep… unconscious. He's okay and on his way to hospital."

Sam flopped into the chair behind her. "Jesus. When is this frigging nightmare going to end? Is Chanters all right?"

"Not really. It sounds to me like he is on the verge of doing something rash."

"What? To himself, is that what you're saying, Bob?"

He shrugged. "Who knows what state of mind he's in? His whole family, what's left of it, is being held captive now."

Sam nodded as the realisation dawned on her. "I get that. The poor man. We need to bring him in. We'll protect him here, if necessary."

Bob frowned and tapped a finger against the side of his face. "Too late for that, isn't it? If the killer's intention was to take the old man, he had the ideal opportunity to do it today."

Sam let out a groan. "You're right. Jesus. Tell me someone has gone around there to comfort him, at least. Does he need medical attention?"

"I asked, he said he was fine. I agree, someone should go round there, although it is a crime scene, so it's going to be packed with SOCO et cetera."

"Suzanna and Liam, that's going to be you. Arm yourself with Tasers before you leave, just in case. Alex, we're going to be calling on your expertise to find that Ford, if that's the car the murderer used. We need to find out where he's taken Fiona and Summer. Bloody hell, could this day get any worse?"

Suzanna and Liam shot out of the room.

Bob stared at her. "Yes, it could, but you don't want to hear my thoughts on that."

Sam closed her eyes. "You think the perp is reaching his endgame, don't you?" She opened them again to find Bob nodding.

"Yep. Hate to say it, but he's doing everything during daylight hours, as though he's goading us, not bothered about being caught. Christ, for someone to attack a copper in the process, too, he's got to have a death wish, surely."

Sam mulled over his words. "I feel so inadequate. I'm fed up with going round in circles and the net not closing in on him."

"What's the answer?"

"We get reinforcements to help us for when he strikes. Saying that, if this is him building up to his endgame then it could be too late to instigate what's needed. Claire, I think you should stay here... Damn, Alex, I need you out in the field with us, but you're too good with the cameras, that has to be our main priority. We need to find the car and see in which direction it's heading. Without that proof, we have nothing."

"I'll stay here and crack on with it then, boss."

"Okay, Oliver, you come with us. We'll leave Claire and Alex to work their magic here. Keep us updated as and when you stumble across anything, guys."

"We will, boss. Good luck," Claire shouted as the three of them tore out of the room.

Sam stopped at the front desk long enough to speak to Nick to apologise for one of his men getting injured and also to request that a couple of patrol cars join them at Fiona's residence.

Once Bob, Oliver and Sam were in the car and en route, Bob asked, "What's the idea of going back there? Isn't that like returning to the scene once the horse has bolted?"

"Probably. I need to action the team on site, get them knocking on doors. Someone must have either seen or heard what was said when the perp took Fiona and Summer from the house."

"Wishful thinking, if you ask me," Bob chuntered.

"I'm willing to listen to other options, so feel free to share what you think we should do next, Bob."

He scratched the side of his face and slunk lower into his seat.

Sam shook her head. "See, it's not so easy, is it?"

"I never said it was. All right, maybe I'm guilty of stating the obvious. Finding the solutions to the problems is what has been lacking throughout this case... through no fault of our own," he added before Sam could pounce on what he'd said.

"I agree. There are some cases when we're going to have our backs against the wall. How many times can you think of where I've gone back to the public for help with a second press conference, eh?"

"Not many, if any at all," Bob admitted.

"Exactly, I'm doing my best to counter what this bastard is flinging at us. It pisses me off that he's one step, sometimes three steps, ahead of us. But I'm doing my darndest to combat that issue. Admittedly, without much success, but it's not for want of trying, I can tell you. Do you think having four people missing from one family isn't affecting me?"

"I didn't say that. It's affecting all of us, I can assure you. We're all busting our guts on this investigation."

"I know. All we need now is to nab the bastard and hope that the family don't get hurt in the crossfire as it were."

"Amen to that," Bob muttered.

"Anything to add, Oliver?" Sam asked, glancing at the young detective sitting in the back seat.

"Not really, boss. I've just come along for the ride."

Sam frowned. "Not the answer I was hoping to hear, Oliver. Feel free to chip in at any time."

"Oh, I will, boss. Thanks for dragging me along."

Bob chuckled at his choice of words, and Sam punched her partner's thigh.

"Oi, you, I could have you for assault."

"Bring it on, matey." Sam laughed.

"Nope, not going to happen because I know you'd tie me into knots with your version of the events."

Sam chuckled. "You're nuts. It's a good job I like you."

She drew up outside Fiona's house to find the SOCO team and Des Markham, the forensic pathologist, already in attendance.

"Hi, Des, I'm surprised to see you here. Can we come closer or do you need us to tog up first?"

"Within reason, come to within a few feet. I was in the area, thought I'd stop by and lend a hand."

"I'm glad you and your team are taking this seriously."

She and Bob shuffled forward while Oliver went off in the other direction, as per Sam's instructions, to start knocking on the neighbours' doors along with the other uniformed officers at the scene, to gather what information was available about the incident.

"How was he attacked, any idea?" Sam asked.

"I managed to give him a quick examination before the paramedics took him away, he was struck from behind with a heavy object. Once he was down on the ground, the perpetrator hit him a couple more times with the intention of killing him. His face took the brunt of the force, it's not pretty."

"I feel responsible. I requested one officer to guard the property. In hindsight, maybe I should have ordered two men to be here instead."

Des shrugged. "Might have saved him from taking a battering, who knows? On the other hand, the perpetrator might have taken two officers out then, instead of only one. Sorry to be such a pessimist, it's the truth."

"I know. It won't stop me feeling guilty, though, all the same."

"That's because you're a sensitive soul with a good heart."

Sam sighed. "It beggars belief the lengths this perp is prepared to go to."

"Are you any closer to finding out who he is and what his motive is?"

"Nope. Now he's kidnapped both sisters, and the husband and baby, as well as killing the mother and leaving Fiona's best friend for dead. She's recovering in hospital, but having long Covid could hamper her progress."

"Are you telling me the body count might rise again?"

Sam looked his way and rolled her eyes. "Most definitely. I'm consciously glancing over my shoulder, just in case."

"Metaphorically speaking, you mean," Des said, frowning.

"Yeah, I suppose so. Either way, this investigation is beginning to take its toll on me and the team. We need answers and we're failing at every turn to find them."

"This isn't like you to be such a defeatist, Sam."

She batted away his concern. "Ignore me. A little self-pity comes with the territory now and again. I'm sure it'll all come good in the end."

"Whenever that may be," Bob grumbled.

"Well, it sounds like it's going to be a team effort. We'll do what we can to help out, of course."

Fiona feared for her baby's life more than her own. She realised they were both in a dismal situation and there was nothing she could do about it. The man had placed a hood over her head and had taken Summer's car seat from her and placed them both in a car. She kept cocking her ear for any sign of noise coming from her daughter, making sure he hadn't dumped her en route.

Is that gravel? The car stopped, and the door slammed. There was a slight pause, then she felt his hand on her arm, tugging at the sleeve of her coat for her to get out. The man remained silent. He hadn't said a word since he'd swept into her house and abducted her. Bile rose in her throat as she relived the scene. The man had somehow got into the house, but how? There had been an officer armed with a Taser, standing guard on the front doorstep. She had no way of knowing if he'd come in the front or the back, he'd just appeared and surprised her and her father. Bless him, her father had done his very best to protect her from being taken, but her kidnapper had battered him until he was too weak to protect himself, let alone Fiona and Summer. She couldn't blame her father for his lack of survival instincts, he was getting on and had been through the mire this week.

The man guided her. She thought she heard a metal gate and wondered if they would be entering a house soon, but no, she was now juddering and going downwards. *Some kind of lift? Are we in a block of flats? What about the gate?* Confused, she tried to concentrate on the sounds her daughter was making. Summer didn't sound distressed at all. At least the man seemed to be taking care of her okay. That was a relief, especially when she'd heard on the news recently that the area was rife with paedophiles. *Don't even go there.*

The juddering came to a halt, and the gate screeched open again. The noise made Summer cry out. The man hushed her with a soothing voice. *Is he disguising his voice? Does he have children? Maybe he'll show us some compassion. Or maybe he's going to sell us both into slavery. No, I shouldn't think that way.*

A door clicked open. "Oh God, Fiona!"

"Donna? Is that you?" Fiona asked, straining an ear in the hood.

The man removed the hood. She rubbed her eyes over and over, unable to adjust to the dimly lit room. Summer was lying unfazed and unharmed in her car seat by her feet. On the other side of the room, her sister sat in a chair, her feet and wrists bound. She rushed towards her. "I'm so glad you're all right. Where are we?"

Donna teared up. She shook her head, clearly shocked. Her eyes drifted upwards behind Fiona. She turned, sensing someone was there.

"Jesus, *Rory*. I'm so glad you're alive. Did he hurt you?" She rose to her feet and moved forward to hug her husband who took a step backwards. At first, she thought he was injured and he didn't want her touching him, but then she saw the hatred filling his eyes and asked, "Why aren't you bound like Donna?"

He tipped his head back and laughed. "Ah, now it's sinking in, isn't it? Why don't we get you more comfortable?" He grabbed her roughly and guided her to a chair, close to her sister.

Fiona was stunned into silence. Even though ten thousand questions or more were running through her fraught mind, her mouth failed to put the questions into words as he trussed her up like a chicken. Eventually, when he'd finally finished tying her feet, she managed to voice one simple word, "Why?"

His grin broadened and his gaze drifted between her and her sister. "Because I could. I've had it with you and your family. You'll perish down here, this place is near enough to Hell. No doubt your mother is already there by now, making the Devil's life hell with her vicious tongue."

"What? You killed her? Did you put Sophie in hospital as well?"

"The penny is well and truly dropping now, isn't it?"

"Why? Why punish us like this when I, we, have all shown you nothing but kindness over the years?"

He laughed again. Summer giggled, wanting to join in the fun. He walked over to the car seat and picked up his child.

No wonder she didn't cry in the car and the lift, she must have recognised her father. God, what if he runs off with her? How are

Donna and I going to get out of here alive? How can I save my family when I'm tied up like this?

Rory returned with Summer. He looked down at his daughter, love etched into his face. "She's the only one who has never let me down. She loves me as much as I love her."

"I love you, Rory, despite all that's gone on between us. Untie me, we can leave here together. Make a new life somewhere else."

Donna gasped. "Why, you selfish bitch. I hate you. You fucking two belong together."

"Carry on, girls, I enjoy a family squabble as much as the next person. And where would we go, *darling wife*?" he asked, his tone laced with sarcasm.

"Anywhere, I just want to be with you. I've barely slept since Sunday. I've missed you so much, Rory. We can do this, make it work, I know we can."

"I don't think so, Fiona. This whole plan was devised so that I'd be able to take Summer and get as far away from you as possible."

Fiona gasped.

Donna sniggered. "Looks like your plan has just bitten you in the arse, sister dearest."

Fiona faced her sister and sneered, "Shut up! You don't know what you're talking about. Keep your opinions to yourself."

"Fine by me. He's going to leave you to rot here, without food and water, and you're still delusional about what state your frigging marriage is in. Get a life, Fiona. Wake up and smell the fucking roses, will you? Jesus, how naïve can one woman be? You definitely come out top on that poll."

"Shut up. You know nothing about our relationship. You... a woman who can't keep hold of a man longer than a couple of weeks."

"You're wrong. It's usually me who dumps them, sis, you want to know why? Because I refuse to let them walk all over me. Men always try to win women over the first few weeks of a relationship, their masks invariably slip after that. The thing is, being a strong woman, I can see through their shenanigans long before they get the chance to turn into something more sinister. Whereas you, you would cling to it, like you have done over the years. You've seen the abuse he's dished out as affection. You're as sick in the head as he is, you just haven't got the courage to admit it."

Fiona wrestled with her chair, eager to get her hands on Donna. "Why you, utter bitch. You know nothing about me and my life. We're happy, aren't we, Rory?"

Rory stood a few feet ahead of Fiona. He stared at her for a couple of moments and then shook his head. "I haven't been happy since the day I married you. All I wanted out of you was a child. Now I have her, my life is complete. Yes, I had to leave her with you while I punished your family and put the rest of my plan into action, but after today, Summer and I will be long gone."

"No, don't say that. I've given up everything to be with you. I've done my very best over the years to make you happy, and this is how you repay me? Take me with you, we can start over again elsewhere. You know how much you mean to me."

"Why would I want to be with a woman I despise? Tell me, I can't wait to hear your reply."

Fiona was lost for words. Her whole world was crumbling around her. The man she thought she loved was intending to walk away and leave her down here in this hellhole, taking their daughter with him. *What am I supposed to say to make things right between us? Will I ever be able to do that?* "Please, Rory, don't do this. I'll change, if that's what you want me to do."

"Into what? A domestic goddess and a whore in the bedroom, like other married women? I'm done with you. I'm going to take Summer and leave."

"No, you can't. I won't allow you to take her," she cried out in desperation.

He took a step forward and whacked her around the face. Fiona cried out, and tears dripped onto her cheeks. She had to fight to keep him talking. She couldn't allow him to leave and take Summer with him, she just couldn't. Her life would be wretched, if she ever got out of here alive.

"You no longer have a say in my life, bitch. Summer will be better off with me. I'll treat her like a princess. Teach her how to act around a man, to respect men and how to love properly without asking for anything in return."

"What? What are you saying? Don't do this. She needs her mother. Don't forget I'm still breast-feeding her," she yelled as an afterthought.

"That can easily be remedied. You can buy formula everywhere nowadays. She'll adjust, lose every tie she's ever had with you. I can raise her, how difficult can it be? You women always make a song and dance out of everything. She has needs, of course she has, but I can deal with them, now she's getting older."

"She's six months old, for fuck's sake," Fiona inadvertently snapped. "She needs her mother more now than ever. You're a fool if you believe raising her on your own will be a breeze."

He grinned and tilted his head. "You're assuming I'll be alone."

"What? Are you telling me you're seeing someone else? Another woman?"

He tapped the side of his nose and smiled. "That secret will go with me."

"How long has this affair been going on? How dare you! I've given you everything I have over the years, not once have I ever looked at another man, and here you are telling me you have another woman on the go. Who is she?"

"Wouldn't you like to know? And don't give me that bullshit about you caring for me the best you could, what bloody dreamworld are you living in?"

Fiona turned to look at Donna. "Did you know about this? Him having an affair?"

Donna screwed up her nose. "Why should I know? I kept out of your marriage, if you can call it that. It was shambolic from the first day, you were too loved-up to see it. He's always treated you like dirt. You should be ashamed of yourself for bringing Summer into this world, into a loveless marriage, and now you and your family are suffering the consequences. You've always been a selfish cow, Fiona. What about our mother's death?"

Fiona's head dropped for a moment, embarrassed, then she came back fighting again. "What are you talking about? We were happy, in the beginning."

"Tragic, that's what you are, you're to be pitied if you believe that. He's been seeing other women behind your back for years. Go on, ask him, see if he'll admit it."

Fiona shifted her gaze back to her husband. "Have you?"

"What does it matter? You were never enough for me. I've got what I wanted, a child, you've outlived your usefulness, not that you ever had any discerning features in the first place."

Fiona shook her head in disbelief as fresh tears fell. "How could you be so heartless? I loved you like no other woman could ever love you, and this is how you repay me."

"In your mind, you did the best, except it was never enough, your wifely skills were lacking from day one. I got bored very quickly. You're an idiot if you couldn't tell. I'm done with this, I don't owe you anything. Say goodbye to your daughter, this is going to be the last time you ever see her."

"No! Please, don't do this. I need her, I need you. I'm nothing without you."

13

"We've had a call," Bob interrupted Sam and Des's conversation at the crime scene.

"I'm listening." Sam's pulse raced at the news. She'd had a feeling all day that something huge was about to happen—it had already, with Fiona and Summer being abducted, but it hadn't been enough to satisfy the gnawing sensation in her gut.

"Someone just contacted the station with some interesting information."

"Jesus, spit it out, Bob, or do I have to torture you to get the details?"

"A tad OTT there, boss." He raised his hand, preventing her rebuttal. "A driver close to Egremont informed the station that a silver Ford Puma was driving erratically, came out of a turning and almost smashed into him on the A595, heading our way."

"Okay, this could be what we've been waiting for. Has the desk sergeant actioned an alert?"

"Yep. It's all in hand at their end. What do you want us to do?"

"We'll get on the road and see if we can intercept it. When did this happen?"

"Around twenty minutes ago."

"Sorry, Des. Duty calls. I'll be in touch soon, I promise."

Des waved her off. "Good luck. I hope you catch the bastard this time."

Sam bolted back to the car and shouted, "So do I. Come on, Bob, stop slacking."

Bob upped his pace, and they both jumped in the car.

Sam sped off towards the A595 going south. "Get on the radio to the station, ask to be informed if one of the patrol cars spots the Ford. We'll take our lead from there."

Bob did as instructed, then sighed. "What if he's got Fiona and Summer with him? He's risking them all getting killed if he gets involved in a police chase. Why bring attention to himself by driving erratically?"

"No idea. Maybe Fiona attacked him while he was driving, tried to force him off the road. Who knows? There's no point in us speculating, not until we find the bloody car."

They were on the outskirts of Whitehaven when one of the patrol cars announced they were right behind the Ford.

"Tell him not to lose him," Sam shouted, and she hit the siren.

"I'm not going to say that, it's stating the obvious, boss."

"All right. Damn, I hate to admit when you're right."

"I usually am," Bob mumbled beside her, earning himself a jab in his thigh. "Ouch! Do you mind keeping your hands on the steering wheel at all times while driving at this speed? You're turning me into a nervous passenger." He pointed up ahead. "There it is."

"Shit, it's on the other side of the dual carriageway. I'm going to have to wait until I can get to the roundabout before I can turn around."

"He could be long gone by then... not what you want to hear, I know."

"Let the patrol car know we're not far away and to keep us updated if they turn off."

Bob relayed the message and received the okay signal in return.

"Where could he be heading?" Sam asked.

"Or coming from, come to that."

"Good shout. Did you notice anyone else in the car as we passed?"

"No, I was concentrating all my attention on the driver. He seemed familiar."

"He does? Think, man, where have you seen him? It could make all the difference to where we're heading. We could get ahead of him."

"How are we likely to do that?"

"All right, there's no need to snap my head off, it was only a suggestion. Keep thinking, Bob. It could be important."

Bob shook his head. "I'm thinking, but nothing is coming to mind."

Sam indicated around the roundabout and put her foot down past the cars that had slowed down once they'd heard the siren behind them. "Get out of the way, idiots. Why block the road like that?" she hissed under her breath.

"Calm down. They did the right thing and pulled over to the side. What's your problem?"

"I'm in a rush to arrest a bloody killer, in case you hadn't noticed, partner."

"I know that. There's no need for you to get more and more worked up about it. Chillax once in a while."

Sam quickly glanced his way and back at the road ahead. "Are you for real?"

She responded by pressing her foot down on the accelerator, in the process, slamming his head against the headrest. "Oops, sorry, forgot myself for a moment there."

The radio sparked into life. "He's turned off to the left, going through Whitehaven, down by Morrisons."

"Shit! That's the last thing we need. It's going to be a nightmare tracking him through town with the traffic getting in our way."

"What's the alternative?"

Sam pulled a face and pressed her foot down heavier on the accelerator.

"He's heading towards the harbour," the officer informed them over the radio. "He's stopped, he's getting out of the car. Crap, he's got the child with him."

"Approach with caution. Do not pin him in a corner," Bob replied.

"Good advice. Well done," Sam praised him.

"Must have learnt something from you over the years. You need to take a left here."

She slowed down as the harbour came into view. "He's got the baby, where's Fiona?"

"Maybe she's in the boot of the car. We won't know until we catch up with them. At least he's come to a standstill and is within our grasp."

Sam tutted. "It seems too easy to me. He's been cunning all the way through this, and now, when it comes to the crunch, he's decided to give himself up? Can't see it myself."

"Who said he's giving himself up? There, the patrol car is on the quay. Fuck, I've just remembered where I recognise him from."

Sam brought the car to a halt and was staring at the man holding the car seat. "Rory Knox! Jesus, what a twisted fucking man. We need to get that baby away from him."

"And how do you propose we do that? He's getting closer to the edge."

"Some form of distraction. Why don't I keep him talking and you sneak up from the back?"

"He's walking towards the harbour wall, won't it be a risk? What if he drops the baby into the water?"

Sam heaved out a breath. "I'm all ears if you've got a better strategy."

Bob shrugged. "I haven't, and we're wasting time."

"I'm aware of that. Okay, duck down, maybe he hasn't spotted you yet. I'll walk over to the right, make sure he follows my movements by talking to him. While he's distracted, you get out of the car and make your move. Take it wide—is there a ledge on the other side of the wall? I can't remember."

"Not that I know of, it's a sheer drop into the sea. My concern remains with the child. Why is he here if his intention isn't to ditch the kid?"

"We'll soon find out. Stick to the plan, make your move when you can. If he dumps the baby, get ready to dive into the harbour."

"What? Are you crazy? It's the middle of winter."

"Which is why the baby has to be saved straight away, no dallying on your part. You hear me?"

"Jesus! All right. Time's a wasting. I'll do it. Just make sure you talk him down before I have to take a dip for the kid."

Sam winked at him. "Have faith in my negotiating skills."

He rolled his eyes.

Sam exited the vehicle and strode towards the other officers. "Hello, Rory. I'm DI Cobbs, I suppose you're aware of that if you've been watching the news bulletins all week. I'm glad to see you're still with us. Fancied a breather from your family, did you?"

His eyes narrowed, and he studied Sam from head to toe. "That's very perceptive of you, DI Cobbs. A lifetime breather!"

"And you can get it, but not this way, Rory. Hand the baby over, I know Summer means the world to you. Can you imagine the fear she's feeling at this moment?"

He glanced down at his daughter. "She seems fine to me. Summer loves spending time with her daddy, don't you, sweetie?"

The baby gurgled with pleasure as Rory smiled at her.

"Why traumatise her? Babies have good memories. She'll remember you putting her in danger, I guarantee it." *I hope the lie works, makes him reconsider.* "Would you want that? Don't you want a peaceful life with your child, Rory?"

He continued to stare down at his child. Sam noticed he wasn't holding any weapons; was he really going to dump his daughter in the sea? He was capable of going to the extreme, he'd proven that over the last week, killing two people, kidnapping the two sisters and putting Fiona's friend in hospital. He didn't answer her, so Sam pressed on. "Don't you want your daughter to grow up knowing how much you love her?"

He stared up at Sam again and shuffled his feet. "Of course I do. It's too late for that, though. After what I've done this week."

"Do you regret your actions, Rory?"

"Not really. They had to be taught a lesson. They think I'm inadequate, unable to look after my family. It's not my fault we got into debt. Babies cost a lot of money, most people aren't aware of just how

To Silence Them

much it takes to kit out a nursery and buy the essentials like a pram et cetera."

"I know you did your best for them and you continue to care about your family, so why don't we go and have a coffee somewhere to discuss where we go from here?"

"You're trying to trick me, just like they have over the years. You have no idea of the anguish they've put me through. Phil was the model father, all I've ever tried to do is match his standards in his family's eyes. I've failed over and over. I couldn't take it any more."

"The final nail in the coffin was when they refused to help pay off your ten grand debt, am I right?"

He mulled over her words for a brief moment then nodded. "Yes. It wasn't much to ask. At least, I didn't think it was. It was for Fiona's and Summer's benefit as well. The pandemic hit my business hard. Yes, it's recovered a little since then, but trade is still slow, people are more cautious with their money—"

His sentence remained incomplete because Bob jumped him. He tore the car seat from his hand, and the two uniformed officers closed in to cuff him. Sam released a relieved sigh and approached the group.

"I knew you'd end up tricking me." Rory spat at her feet. "You're just like all the others. But I still have the upper hand, you'll never find the sisters, not until it's too late. They'll run out of air in days." He bit down on his tongue, and his gaze drifted away from Sam's.

She realised then, that he'd said more than he'd intended. "Where are they? You might as well tell us. If you come clean, I'll do what I can for you with the Crown Prosecution Service, but it will ultimately be up to the judge."

He laughed. "Nice try. Nope, it ain't gonna happen. I'll go to my grave never divulging where they are."

"I've heard enough. Take him away," Sam instructed the two officers who guided Rory back to the patrol car.

Sam stared down at the gurgling Summer. "We'll need to get in touch with Social Services to care for the baby for now, won't we?" Bob asked.

"Yes, I don't suppose her grandfather will be up to looking after her, the state he's in. Make the call, Bob." Sam took the car seat from him and ran her hand around the child's face, her maternal instinct appearing from nowhere, surprising even her. Tears welled up, and she swiped them away. She was just about to sit on a nearby bench when her mobile rang. "Excuse me a moment, Summer." She answered the call, "DI Cobbs, how can I help?"

"It's Claire, boss. I've just received a call from a member of the public regarding the silver Ford Puma."

"I'm going to stop you there, Claire. We've got them, the baby is fine. You'll never guess who was behind it all."

"Thank God. Who?"

"Rory Knox."

"Shit! That's unbelievable. But, boss, I've got further news regarding the vehicle."

Sam's spirits rose. "Hit me with it."

"A man called to say he saw a car resembling the Ford in the Egremont area. He said he saw a man, woman, and a child in a car seat he thought it was, all heading towards one of the old mineshafts in the area."

They'll run out of air in days – Rory's hateful words reverberated through her head.

"Boss, boss, are you still there?"

"Yes, sorry. I was recalling what Rory said when I pleaded with him to tell me where Donna and Fiona are being held. He said they'll run out of air soon. Look, I'm not prepared to sit back on this one, Claire. Get all the teams you can gather to the location. Bob and I will get there as soon as we can, we've got Summer's welfare to consider first. Keep me informed."

"I'll arrange everything now. Be in touch soon, boss."

Sam ended the call and rushed back to the car where Bob was sitting in the passenger seat. "Any luck?"

"Yes, someone is going to meet us. I'm just arranging a time and place."

"Try and hurry things along. We've got a possible lead on where Donna and Fiona are being kept."

"Jesus. Okay. Shouldn't we take the child with us in that case? It's not like she's going to be in danger with her father now on his way to the station."

"Excellent point. Secure the car seat in the back of the car. Tell Social Services we'll get back to them within the hour. I believe we should have located Summer's mother by then."

"Will do." Bob ended the call a few moments later. "They weren't happy, but that's tough shit. Christ, it's all happening today, isn't it?"

"It is that. I need to make a personal call to my mother. Ask her to look after Sonny for me, I think we're going to be in for a long one today."

He eyed her suspiciously. "Shouldn't you be calling Chris instead of your mother?"

Sam's cheeks flared under his gaze. "No. Don't ask, leave it there for now, partner. I need to concentrate on the job in hand."

"Sounds like something serious is going on between you two. I'm here if you need to chat."

"Not right now." She tapped her mother's name on the screen of her mobile in its cradle on the dashboard, and her mother answered.

"Hello, Samantha. How are you? Oh no, I forgot to let you know how we got on at the vet's."

"Hi, Mum. Not to worry, I've been up against it here anyway. What did the vet say?"

"That Sonny's paw was badly injured and he needs to rest it for a few days."

"Poor baby. Is he still with you?"

"Yes, he was feeling sorry for himself, I didn't have the heart to drop him back to your place. You can pick him up on the way home, how's that?"

Sam let out a relieved sigh. "That would be fantastic, thanks so much, Mum. It could be a late one as things are kicking off around here."

"What about Chris? Can he pick up Sonny if you're going to be working late? It's not right having a dog and working all the hours you do."

"I know your views, Mum. I'll get something organised in the future so I don't have to depend on you when duty calls and I'm forced to work late."

"I repeat, what about Chris? There are two of you living in that house. It's about time he pulled his weight around the home. I'm repeating myself on that front as well, aren't I?"

Sam closed her eyes and rested her forehead on the steering wheel under her partner's watchful gaze. "Yes, Mum. I'll fill you in later."

"I'll look forward to hearing the excuses you make for him this time. Goodbye, Sam."

"Thanks, Mum, it is appreciated. See you later when I pick Sonny up."

"And don't go turning up at midnight, you hear me?"

"Yes, Mum."

Bob tutted. "Damn, I thought my mum went overboard when she has a point to make. I think your mother takes first prize on that front. Are you sure everything is all right at home?"

"No. It's not. But it's too raw to speak about, besides, we have two women to rescue. Buckle up and hold tight."

"Don't forget there's a baby on board."

Sam brought the car to a screeching halt behind several patrol cars outside the mineshaft. Bob had tried different numbers during the journey in an attempt to try to trace the owners of the mine but drew a blank. It wasn't until they arrived and asked some of the locals who were busy rubbernecking the scene that the owner's name came out. Bob placed the call and arranged for the owner to come down and meet them.

Nigel Wilson appeared shocked when he noticed the mineshaft's opening had been tampered with. "What in the blazes has been going on around here? Who are all these people?"

Sam showed the irate man her ID and filled him in the best she could. "You see, it's imperative we get in there and see for ourselves if the women are still down there."

"Okay, I can take you. Only *two* of you, if we all go the shaft will collapse."

There was a female officer on hand to look after Summer. Sam and Bob grabbed a couple of safety helmets from Nigel, followed him into the rickety old lift and started their descent.

"We need to be careful, any loud noise and this place could come down on us."

"It's okay, we understand the severity of the situation," Sam whispered. Her stomach tied itself into knots the lower they travelled into the dark abyss.

Bob flicked on the penlight torch he kept in his pocket to ease their anxiety in the confined space. Sam broke out in a sweat, her claustrophobia kicking in. In her haste to get to the women, she'd pushed her own paranoia aside for the time being.

"Are you all right?" Bob murmured.

"I will be once we're out in the fresh air again." She closed her eyes, but the sensation of helplessness made her feel ten times worse.

Bob grabbed hold of her arm. "You're safe as long as I'm beside you, Sam."

She smiled and said, "You're my hero."

The lift juddered to a stop, and Nigel led the way through the small tunnel to a door at the rear. He tried the handle. The room was locked. "Damn. I never lock this door. This must be where the women are being kept. I'm going to have to break it down and hope for the best."

"What? But you said we needed to be careful." Sam's fear surged to another level, and she clung to Bob's jacket sleeve.

"Don't worry. He wouldn't risk it if he didn't think he'd get away with it, at least I hope he wouldn't. Hang tight."

Two almighty shoves from Nigel's well-placed shoulder, and the door gave in. Bob and Nigel rushed into the room to rescue the two women who were both tightly bound and gagged.

Sam smiled at the women to try to reassure them. "You're safe now. We have Rory in custody."

"What about Summer, where is she?" Fiona asked the second the gaffer tape was torn from her mouth.

Sam was relieved to find them both safe. "She's outside, waiting for her mummy."

Fiona broke down then. Sobbed so hard it hurt Sam to witness the trauma she was going through. She flung an arm around Fiona's shoulders.

"Come now, there's no need for tears, you're safe, and Rory is behind bars where he belongs."

"I know, but it won't bring our mother back."

Donna nodded. "That's going to be the hardest part, dealing with her funeral in the next few days. Fiona, I'm sorry for what I said in front of Rory, it wasn't intentional, it was my way of trying to get us out of a fix, and it backfired."

"I know you didn't mean any of it. But every word you said was true. I should never have got involved with him in the first place. I'll never trust another man as long as I live."

Sam squeezed Fiona's shoulders as Bob freed her legs from their confines. "Never is a very long time."

EPILOGUE

The rest of the day was spent ensuring Fiona and Donna got the medical attention they needed, along with Summer. The mother-and-daughter reunion was one of the most heartfelt and emotional moments Sam had ever encountered during her career on the force. Once that was all sorted, she turned her attention to interviewing Rory Knox. He surprised her by not going down the 'no comment' route during the hour-long interview. He was charged with one murder, two counts of attempted murder, one count of GBH on the father, and three counts of kidnapping before he was sent to the remand centre.

After ringing the hospital to check the status of the officer who'd been attacked by Rory and receiving the good news that there was every indication he'd make a full recovery after a few weeks recuperation, Sam and her team wrapped the day up with a quick celebratory drink over at the Red Lion, across the road from the station.

"Do you need to have that chat now, you know, about what's going on at home?" Bob whispered in her ear as they waited for the drinks at the bar.

"No. Let's forget about that for now and rejoice in the fact the investigation turned out for the best, in the end. It could have easily gone awry if Rory had got away from us."

"I'd rather not think about that." He shuddered. "I was dreading plummeting into the icy waters after the kid if he'd dropped her in the harbour."

"But you would have done it all the same, because you have a heart of gold and you're a true hero, Bob, wouldn't you?"

He chewed on his lip, paused, then nodded. "All right, I admit it. I would have pushed through the doubts and saved the day."

"You're one of life's good guys."

They carried the drinks over to the table.

Sam joined in the jovial banter flying around for the next thirty minutes then announced her departure. "I'll see you guys first thing in the morning. We'll get this case tied up before the next one lands on my desk. Have a good evening, and thanks for all your hard work with solving the investigation."

She left the pub and darted into the car, narrowly avoiding getting soaked. "Damn rain, when are you going to bloody end?"

Ten minutes later, she drew up outside her parents' detached house. The curtains twitched, and Sonny stood up on his hind legs, peering out of the window. She used her key to enter the house, and he was there to greet her, hobbling on his poorly front paw.

"You're earlier than I thought you would be. Would you like to stay for dinner? It's beef casserole, there's plenty to go around," her mother said, leaning against the doorframe to the lounge.

"I'll pass on that, if you don't mind, Mum. I'd better get this one home, he'll need his walk."

"Nonsense, let him have a rest for a few days. It's no good taking him out in the rain if his paw is still bad, and the vet advised against it to help the paw heal quicker."

"Okay. But I still need to get home."

"What's going on with you and Chris? Don't try and pull the wool over my eyes either. I can tell when a marriage is in trouble, and yours clearly is."

"It's something we have to figure out for ourselves, Mum. I'll let you know when that happens."

"In other words, you want me to keep my nose out of your business."

Sam smiled. "My marriage at least. Thanks for picking up Sonny and looking after him today."

"He's adorable. Look after him and yourself, love. I'm always here if you need me."

Sam kissed her mother on the cheek and hugged her. "Thank you. I needed to hear that." She unhooked Sonny's lead from the coatrack and left the house.

Her mother waved her off on the doorstep.

Sam drove home but couldn't resist stopping off at the park on the way. *What if Rhys is here? What if he isn't? Will I be disappointed?*

Not knowing what she was going to walk into at home only confused her even more. She rummaged in the side pocket in the door and found a plastic bag which she slipped over Sonny's paw. "Come on, boy, just a quick one in between the showers."

Sonny hopped out of the car, not caring if his paw was hurting or not. She knew then she'd made the right decision, taking the detour to the park. She let him off the lead, and he chased the squirrels up several of the nearby deciduous trees. Sam glanced around, constantly on the lookout for Rhys, but he was nowhere to be seen. A few minutes later, when she had drifted off into a world of her own, debating what to do about her marriage, a hand tapped her shoulder. She spun around, her palm slapped over her heart, and smiled. "Frighten a girl to death, why don't you?"

"Didn't you hear me call out your name?" Rhys returned her smile.

"If I had I would have turned around."

"Where were you?"

She winked and sniggered. "Standing right here."

"It's good to see you smiling. I meant, you were deep in thought; any specific reason?"

"Not really. I suppose I was contemplating my day at work."

He inclined his head. "Don't stop there."

"We caught a killer who had faked his own kidnapping, killed his mother-in-law, assaulted his father-in-law and his wife's best friend,

M A COMLEY

who ended up in hospital with serious injuries, kidnapped his sister-in-law, his wife and his own daughter, plus he also assaulted a serving policeman who was guarding the family home."

"Wow, you're amazing. What was his motive? Or is he pleading insanity or going down the 'no comment' route?"

"He did the latter but not before he told me why he'd set out on the path he'd gone down. It was all about the family letting him down. He had a debt, and none of them were willing to lend him the cash."

"Jesus, so it was all about revenge?"

"About sums it up. He'll be locked up for life, I'll make sure of that."

"Good for you. And how are things at home?"

A cloud swept over her, dimming her good mood. "Let's change the subject because I haven't got a scooby doo."

He cradled her cheek in his hand. "I'm here for you. Just remember that."

"Thank you. I have to get Sonny home now."

He pecked her on the cheek, and they parted company. Sam drove home to find the house in darkness. Her heart shattered into a million pieces. Chris was gone.

Will he ever come back? Do I even care?

THE END

Thank you for reading the second book in the DI Sam Cobbs series, you'll be pleased to know that book three is now available. To Make Them Pay.

Until then, maybe you'd also like to try one of my edge-of-your-seat thriller series. Grab the first book in the best-selling Justice here, **Cruel Justice**

Or the first book in the spin-off Justice Again series, **Gone in Seconds.**

*P*erhaps you'd prefer to try one of my other police procedural series, the DI Kayli Bright series here, **The Missing Children.**

*O*r maybe you'd enjoy the DI Sally Parker series set in Norfolk, UK. **WRONG PLACE.**

*A*lso, why not try my super successful, police procedural series set in Hereford. Find the first book in the DI Sara Ramsey series here. **No Right To Kill.**

*T*he first book in the gritty HERO series can be found here. **TORN APART**

*O*r why not try my first psychological thriller here. **I Know The Truth**

KEEP IN TOUCH WITH M A COMLEY

Pick up a FREE Justice novella by signing up to my newsletter today.
https://BookHip.com/WBRTGW

BookBub
www.bookbub.com/authors/m-a-comley

Blog
http://melcomley.blogspot.com

Why not join my special Facebook group to take part in monthly giveaways.

Readers' Group

Printed in Great Britain
by Amazon